The Sudden Death of …..

Serge Gavronsky

Spuyten Duyvil
New York City

copyright 2008 Serge Gavronsky
ISBN 1-933132-65-5

Library of Congress Cataloging-in-Publication Data

Gavronsky, Serge.
The sudden death of-- / Serge Gavronsky.
p. cm.
ISBN 978-1-933132-65-5
1. Poets--Death--Fiction. I. Title.
PS3557.A957S83 2008
813'.54--dc22
2008012468

Professor Serge Gavronsky died last night of a seizure. According to his long-time friend, David Gordon, Professor Gavronsky swallowed his tongue before anyone could save him. When he died, looking out the window of his bedroom, clouds passed by quickly, like white caps on rapid moving waves heading for shore.

(At four you could hear traffic snarl below on West End Avenue. Once in a while sirens. Were they fire trucks or ambulances?)

A quiet settled down in the bedroom, covered by shelves and shelves of books.

When he was taken away on a stretcher, no one took the time to make his bed. It remained as it had been: 2 pillows fallen on the floor, sheets thrown about, two blue winter blankets on the green carpet.

Shortly thereafter, two policemen rang the door bell, came in. They were offered something to drink. The first one refused: "We're not supposed to drink anything on the job." The second one happily accepted. "A soda if you've got it?"

They looked at the old upright piano, the Chagall print above it and a portrait over the massive oak credenza.

Outside the sun set. Nature's clock.

On Riverside Drive women watered their garden and at the opposite end of the walk, a Holocaust memorial where others dawdled over their baby carriages, smiling, playing with attached Calder-like toys hanging on the top. Some babies smiled. Others cried.

Young fathers rested their bikes while three others, in skin tight outfits and post-modern racing helmets, zoomed down the hill, heading for the boat basin. When they got to the tunnel they struck up their usual speed under the tunnel. One of them yoddled just to make sure he was there.

As far as anybody was concerned, after ample tears shed, hand-wringling, memories evoked, others sat down on the beaten-up couch while still others sat in armchairs which also had seen better days. On the cocktail table, a copy of Friday's "Le Monde," the one with book reviews.

From the kitchen, you could hear the hissing of the kettle.

Porcelain tea cups were laid out on a tray and then carried through the poorly painted hinged door to the living room.

After a decent amount of time, friends dispersed as did the two policemen.

According to Professor Gordon, teaching French at UPSD, Professor Gavronsky was a well-known translator of contemporary French poetry, a poet himself, and an authority on Négritude, a course he inaugurated in 1968 when BOSS (Barnard Organization of Soul Sisters), charged into the chairman's office, 107, Milbank Hall, and insisted that another literature existed apart from that White Stuff the department had been feeding its students ever since the founding of the college in 1889.

A colleague remembers Professor Gavronsky as a friendly person, ready to encourage his students, help them on their Senior Essays and write letters of recommendations for those hoping to get into a graduate faculty.

But according to Professor Gordon, much more can be said about Professor Gavronsky whose untimely death at the age of 73 brought tears to many who knew him.

A 1954 graduate of Columbia College, he had majored in European History and minored in French. In his major, he had worked with Richard Hofsteader and, in particular, with Jacques Barzun, soon to be appointed Provost of Columbia University at the difficult moment when students rebelled against the central administration.Took over some buildings: Havermeyer, Math and Grayson Kirk's presidential office in Low Library. Everybody remembers the student who borrowed one of Kirk's cigars, and leaned out the window. That provided him those fifteen minutes of fame.

A little appreciated New York "Times" reporter was asked to check into Gavronsky's Google entries. As a result, a huge and at times repetitive entries came up as if a certain bibliographic vomit had swollen in the journalist's throat. Perhaps his penchant for cappuccino helped in this particular instance to liberate all metaphors so greedily hoarded by this same journalist in other columns. His well-clipped mustache. The publication found most appealing though certainly not the first entry was the U of California Press The Power of Language, something which had tempted the journalist ever since he had begun, as a novice, at the paper.There he found a lengthy presentation of the work of Francis Ponge whom he remembered from his college days, not that long ago. In that moment of reminiscence, he recalled that poet anti-poet, that materialist, that rejector of Romantic poetry and who called Jacques Prévert the accordionist on the corner. He shuffled his memory and rememebered Ponge's technique, a lesson for any one writing. Locate words in the Littré, list them as part of the work in progress: "Learn from language." What an odd person. He thought to himself put down place and date. In truth he actually believed that they constituted his form of painting or perhaps more, as in a Chinese scroll he had purchased in Seoul, proof of his capacities to draw ideograms. He became such a specialist in Gavronsky's work, that the managing editor of the city desk sent him to Paris to look further into Gavronsky's life, even if he hadn't lived there for a long time. Let's say until the Nazi bombers threatened the Luxembourg gardens and huge sandbags had been placed all around "important" statues, a bit like what had happened to major churches and monuments in Paris: for example, the column in front of what remained of the Bastille.

He discovered that, as a boy in the Luxembourg gardens, Gavronsky had floated his sailboat and pushed it off the side with a long stick. He then wore blue shorts, a short sleeve white shirt, and shoes his mother had bought him on rue de Rennes.

When the war threatened his family, his mother, a lawyer, was insistently asked by the "batonnier" (the president of the bar) to stay in Paris even though she thought she would have been one of the first, as a Jew, to be sent to a French prisoners's of war camp like Les Milles outside of Aix where, by the way, not a single sign indicated its emplacement today.

The "Times" journalist had never encountered such incivility, he coming from Memphis, from a sound Protestant family, having gotten a scholarship to go to Harvard where he majored in English. No doubt that helped him get a job. Muttering to himself, sitting at a side-walk café on bld St. Germain (was it Old Navy?) what a treat it had been when he read Hard Times. His high school friend at Columbia had been fascinated by Lionel Trilling's analysis of that same novel as well as Virginia Woolf's To the Lighthouse (OOOPs, he corrected himself and immediately punishing himself, added something like Crime and Punishment). No matter, literature was literature and Virginia belonged to it.

He discovered that, at the lycée Fénelon, Gavronsky's mother had befriended that other Russian Jew, Nathalie Sarraute, with whom she kept in contact for the rest of their lives. In fact, Sarraute had written (of course handwritten!) a long letter describing what the war years had been like as well as the post-war situation. The letter ended with a call for her best friend to return to Paris even though their apartment had been squatted, his mother's office stripped bare of everything: books, paintings etc. His father's dental office was unrecognizable. Everything had disappeared even the mirror. (Gavronsky had read that letter at an NYU conference on Sarraute two years before the journalist had begun his research.) To help him write an informed obituary, he succeeded in hiring an "informant," as anthropologists call them. He thought that sounded a bit like a traitor's job. He found out that "grand-père" lived on rue Boulard, perpendicular to rue Daguerre where famous people lived like Claude somebody, a well-known translator and poet in his own right. He was struck by the disappearance of street vendors, those who yelled "mes jolis abricots" or "achetez mes belles tomates." It probably would take another journalist to do that street justice.

"Grand-père," as it turned out (the informer was particularly helpful in this matter) when he got to Paris, bulged his cellar with all the newspapers he could find. To help those Socialist Russian émigrés, he organized recitals, dances (Pavlova was one of his favorites) and the informer thought Chaliapin may also have sung in the Workers' Hall.

Was it known that, as a young man, "grand-père" had been sent to Siberia? Kerensky had been his lawyer, to no avail. When the first revolution occurred, Kerensky named him Mayor of Moscow which "grand-père" refused to accept because he was Jewish, his own father, a Rabbi in Wilna, the rabbi would have caused a flurry of protest and so Kerensky named him to the Duma.

The journalist, looking at himself in the toilet mirror of the Deux Magots or was it the one next door? noticed the stain on his British elbow patch and feared that it might have gone right through to his button-down Brooks Bros. shirt, the one with an upright sheep on the front pocket.

But the great discovery, a discovery no one would have made had they not deepened their knowledge of Gavronsky's stay in Paris, years after the war, was a hand-written manuscript, the edges having been nibbled away by hungry rats, a bit like Charles Fourrier's in Grenoble.

The discovery was so titillating that he found himself reading Gavronsky's own unfinished novel *A Matter of Identity*, thinking that the novel might have revealed something about Gavronsky's life.

The 1968 "events" at Berkeley and Columbia soon spread to Turkey and Japan where similar revolts occurred. At that time, Professor Gavronsky, together with other members of the Barnard faculty (but not that many) ringed Low Library, ready to repel jocks' efforts to overthrow students' machinations. Professor Gavronsky, then a recently promoted assistant professor, spent the early evening in professor James's brownstone off 100th street, then living with his wife, a Barnard graduate, and there awaited for a student to call just in case Grayson Kirk had requested the presence of NYC police. Professor Gavronsky vividly remembered, after an anguished phone call from Professor James' student, that, walking up Broadway, the side streets were blocked by commandeered NY city buses. In his statement to the Columbia "Spectator," Professor Gavronsky remembered running up the stairs to Low Library, to ring Low Library against the onslaught of Columbia jocks who, with loud speakers in hand, promised to dislodge all students who had taken over Columbia buildings. Professor Juviler, of the Political Science department at BC, clearly remembered, thirty years later, how all the-then faculty joined hands in a vain effort to protect Columbia and Barnard students from police attacks. They not only succeeded in thwarting the Jocks' plans to storm Low Library, but also on the lawn fronting Ferris Booth Hall where they tried to protect their own students from the police cavalry, sweeping up the ceremonious stairs of Low Library, hitting students with their billies. At that moment, professor Gavronsky spotted one of his students, hit by the police and hysterically crying. He escorted her to Chock Full O' Nuts on the corner of 116th Street, where they drank sour coffee and ordered raisin bread with cream cheese.

According to the following morning's obituary in the New York "Times," Professor Gavronsky came from a long line of illustrious members of his family. In the eighteenth century, count Vladimir Gavron owned 3000 serfs who were emancipated in 1861 by the tzar. Some of his freed serfs claimed that name for themselves as a prefix to their newfound identities and so it was, at least so says a manuscript found in Tel Aviv, that the name Gavronsky was coined. Others have suggested the name came from the Gavron River, separating Poland from Russia and, still others, knowing Serbo-Croatian, insisted that Gavron was a raven in that language. Those who adhered to that theory jokingly recited Poe's poem, to underline the connection. Nothing was ever proven and, in the following century, and right down to the twentieth, the Gavronskys led an exemplary life. Serge Gavronsky, born in 1932 in Paris or rather in Boulogne-sur-Seine, on the outskirts of Paris, always insisted that, with a dentist grand father, practicing in Moscow, such anterior associations were illegitimate. In the dental case, he managed to treat members of the Bolshoi company. Because of that, his son, Gavronsky's father, at the age of 5 was lucky enough to assist in a rehearsal of Chekhov's "Three Sisters," with the playwrite in the audience. Victor Gavronsky, who himself was to follow in his father's footsteps, had the unforgettable pleasure of hearing Chaliapin sing, Pavlova dance and, in the great music hall, listen to Casadesus playing Chopin's Prelude Number 3 written shortly after his trip to Italy with that pipe-smoking George Sand. Victor Gavronsky, Serge's father, had not meant to become a dentist, however talented he became. As a graduate of the Gymnasium, the only Jew there, and the one who walked away with all the prizes ranging from Latin, Greek, European literature to the history of Russian peasantry under Alexander I. He would have continued, having already begun his research in Geneva's famed library, but his father, insisting that his son earn a living, forced him to go to Paris and enroll in medical school: which he did. It is said that among his patients there was a famous WWI spy, a woman who had shown great courage in gathering secret information in Berlin. Serge Gavronsky's maternal grandmother was the only member of the family to escape the Nazi invasion and come to New York where she lived for three more years before her death, on 107th street and Amsterdam Avenue on a fifth floor walk-up apartment. Serge Gavronsky's uncle, a doctor, may have been the very last to make night visits to Russian immigrants in Queens. With his coat slung over his shoulder, he would drive his 1947 Ford to anywhere he was called, and he continued to do exactly that until his eightieth birthday. He was celebrated with all the bottles of champagne his patients could find over the years. His wife, "tante"Gaby, tried to go back to sleep but, as she had often said, she couldn't until "Oncle" Choura came back. Their two daughters perfectly succeeded in their lives. One married her math teacher at the Lycée Français and settled in Paris before divorcing that man; the other sister became a dancer and danced on impossible stages throughout the US with the Marquis de Cuavas company, on movie stages, totally unfit for classical dance or any other dancing, for that matter. She had gone to Music and Art and every birthday, invited all of her friends to that unfashionable apartment where her mother, the night before, had made a "macédoine," to the great pleasure of all the young guests who had never tasted a cold preparation of small peas, beets, chopped up carrots, cucumbers and a sauce made up of mayonnaise and Dijon mustard.

There is less information about the maternal side but there was a fascinating footnote to her story. In 1940, a low level US State Department counselor knocked on her door and informed her that FDR had personally signed a paper according US visas to all Jewish revolutionaries who would clearly be killed the day the Nazis took over Paris. The names had been turned over by the American Jewish Congress. Maternal grand-mother laughed. Her husband had died in 1932! The low level functionary, Joseph Greenstein, insisted, turned to her and said: "Still, you can go to the US all by yourself!" He smiled, thinking at least he had succeeded in saving one if not two Jews. Maternal grand-mother replied " I'll go if you issue visas to my daughter, her husband and their two children; my son, his wife and their two kids." And thus a whole family was saved by a dead man.

Adam Adams, the NY "Times" bureau chief in New York, and a sometime contributor to the "New Yorker" (read his in-depth analysis of the Greek takevover of Chateau Margaux), was so hypnotically intrigued by the idea of the obit that he inadvertently turned the page to DISTINCTIVE HOMES: Capital Properties & Estates. He was momentarily struck by the 10 million dollar mansion located in Bellmead, NJ with its raised stone patio, 4 BRs and 4 baths and a granite kitchen, all five minutes away from Princeton. Retired French Professor, Léon-François Hoffman's wife was in the real estate business. Adam Adams wondered if she had had anything to do with that prospective sale, not that he would have been able to purchase it, but he could dream about settling there with his wife, three children and a Swedish baby sitter.

Part of Adam Adams's responsibilities was to go further, biographically speaking, into the deceased husband's life.

In 1898, the political chief of the Moscow Police was killed. After a meticulous search, nothing was found to incriminate anyone even though the Police had been given a great deal of latitude including mild torture of all political prisoners in the central jail in Moscow. Finally, and to the Tzar's insistence, all university students who had ever attended a political rally had to be rounded up. Minor, SG's grandfather, was jailed. He did manage to have Kerensky plead his case in court but to no avail and the young man was sent to Siberia on foot with many phenomenal attempted escapes by women prisoners. They crossed Lake Baikal, a huge, ocean-wide lake, singing songs about it and finally arrived at a barracks camp. The young man was assigned to a large room with common criminals who had been given a heavy dose of comic books to keep them quiet. The young university student read them Crime and Punishment: the prisoners were enthralled. At five o'clock the next morning all were summoned to breakfast. The young university student found the ear, neck and goiter soup so disgusting (having eaten caviar with a soup spoon in his own home) that he nearly puked. A long-term prisoner told him to watch his thumb. If he hit it with a hammer in order to insert dynamite in the rocks he would certainly maim himself for life. The counsel was well taken. Returning to the mess hall at 12 he was so famished that he ate whatever was served.

At night, after lights out, the conversation turned to Marx, Engels, Trotsky and at rarer times to Kerensky himself. In this manner a young university student became a revolutionary. When the Tzar's wife gave birth to a baby boy, the university student was sent to a village in Siberia where, in semi-liberty, he began taking notes on the stars and sending them back to a Moscow newspaper.

"Fred, you've got a phone call from NY. I think I know the voice: your boss, Adam, managing editor of the city desk. Talk to him."

" What's up?"

"You're getting me bored with all that shit information. Get something hot. Make Gavronsky a human being. Try. I know you can dig up stuff."

Fred slammed down the receiver. "What about another buttered 'tartine'?

 and an espresso. Where the hell am I going to dig up his private parts?"

A little voice in the back of his attentive mind suggested he try the concierge at 107 Bld. Raspail, the last place Gavronsky had bunked down with a French government fellowship. The taxi was in the middle of bld Montmartre in front of the café Dôme. He jumped in. "Take me around the corner to 107 Raspail." In no time he was there, ran to see the concierge in her box, right off the entrance. "Concierges," he muttered to himself, "were put there as spies. Was it by Napoléon or somebody else like Napoleon III, right before he decided to invade Mexico?"

He knocked on her box. The fat lady, who stank of overcooked cabbage, came out. "Jeune homme, que voulez-vous?" She inquired in her lockjawed French. Perhaps lithium... "Madame, Serge Gavronsky lived in the maid's room on the 7th floor about six years ago. Do you remember him?"

"Comment l'oublier!"

"I guess he also had a basement locker. Can you take me there? I'm a journalist, trying to get info on him."

Down in the basement, filled with old bikes, rotten trunks, a couple of split valises, there, when she opened his locker, a slew of tied-up letters fell out. He immediately began to write down everything he could decipher and, pencil in hand, wrote on a small writing pad he had bought at the Prix Unis on rue de Rennes. He read the first letter.

"Darling, where the hell are you? I've been jerking off just thinking of you, your affirmative nipples, held your pubic hair you sent me in an enveloppe two weeks ago. Then nothing, not a glimmer of hope. Where are you? Are you thinking of me? Have you too, slipped a delicate and anxious hand up your pyjamas and slowly started you know what. Is the mattress still as aweful? Tell me. I'm writing to you from a distant land. Here I can hear the roar of imaginary lions. I can imagine ants crawling into my bed, a disgusting, low sort of a bed. But the only thing saving me is you. Do you remember when we sat facing the statue of Joan of Arc and you caressed me and held a handkerchief over my cock until I came. God knows how I wished I could have come inside you, a fulfilling experience. Don't you agree? Then I'd kiss your open mouth. Tongues would meet. Hands move over your body until—well, I think so—you too got wet inside that Victoria's Secret. I kiss you all over the place. Please write."

Fred lifted another letter, this time in her writing.

"Darling...of course I remember, but you seem to have forgotten that my room mate, Jane, had just come in when we were about to fuck on my cushy bed...I got up, closed the door.

Judy-I could see her now-nodding her head went straight for the toilet. She didn't have a boyfriend at that time. The only thing she wanted was a threesome. Do you remember? You took pity on her. Asked her to come in. She stripped as fast as she could. Shut the light off (we loved seeing each other naked in the mirror on the back wall!) Judy jumped in the middle and started touching both of us at the same time. I think she enjoyed me more than you! Her hand caressed my tits. Her mouth over my nipples, her hand gently moving down to my crack. Sorry if I'm using such technical language. She slipped her finger in me and started moving until I came. Then she lowered herself and started licking my cunt, hoping I'd come again. In the meantime, do you remember? You asked her to get on her knees, hands on the bed, and you, with an ample supply of vaseline, pushed your cock up her ass, started moving in and out, and I could feel her tingling, moving with your rhythm, catching your cock and not letting go! I guess you loved that, and when you shot your load into her open flesh, you asked her to turn around so you could lick her. All three of us were having a great time! I must tell you that, when you disappeared with your French government fellowship and told me you'd be gone for a whole semester, I couldn't do without all of that sex fun and so...Please forgive me, but I'm about to get married. You don't know Timothy but he comes from a Connecticut family. He's already taken me to meet his parents. We played two sets of tennis on his own court then, all heated up, we jumped into his pool. You'll never guess but underwater he managed to strip me and off he went, plunging his rod into me! I said, what a surprise, and he said what about making this a real thing? His hands were all over me and, because the water was warm and the sun shown down on us, I agreed. So we're getting married in two weeks! You can imagine the wedding! A rabbi standing under the old apple tree with the pool in the background and, after saying his inaudible prayers, we all aimed for the banquet tables. Champagne gushed out from ten bottles, the best, Veuve

Cliquot (I told him I loved that and gave him the year I preferred, a 1978). Emma Bovary couldn't have had a better deal! We gouged ourselves on salmon, caviar (I ate it with a soupspoon!) and so much else I can't remember. But you would have died, or at least, knowing your stomach, been sick for days! Then, well then, he slipped his hands under my blousy white skirt, lifted me up, and went straight to the bedroom, one of 10 in the mansion. You can guess what happened next, but I must tell you your hands were on my skin, you in me. Actually, with all the champagne he had drunk, he couldn't even get a decent erection. "So sorry," he said. "Next time, I promise…" In fact, it seems that he always had another excuse like he had just spent a sleepless night on the Red Eye or a flight from London. You name it and you'll see why I come on my own, sometimes even resorting to the handle of my hair brush. Imagine that!

Love to you and I really hope you'll get some fine flesh in Paris!"

The letter over, he put it to his nose and thought she had either doused it with perfume or actually wiped herself with it.

Fred flipped. "That'll make him into a human being, just like they do in novels."

PAUSE

"With her right hand on the wheel and lowering the window with her left, she screamed at me: "You rich prick in that Jag."

That's the way I left the parking lot "centre ville," Southampton, founded in 1664.

However, the going had been smooth coming in from Westhampton. The gorgeous ancient trees lining the entrance to the town (very old), the "stately" mansions (a cliché) behind those ancient trees. Then the massive church to the right with its enticing "IN" and "OUT." Was it meant for cars, for church goers, for hearses? Not clear, at least for me. On the grounds I saw three large tents with kids playing below them. Was it a preview of Sunday School or games to get kids accustomed to going to church?

"Und mine muttersprach which, in fact, I had lost: Sprachlosen mund." Michael Thalheimer had written (of course…): "speechlessness …manifests itself in an overabundance of words" (director of the Lessing play performed so brilliantly at BAM last week). Was he thinking of his play or my mother tongue, or again the fate of this novel? Who knows.

"Whenever we are trying to recover a recollection, to call up some period of an act sui generis by which we detach ourselves from the present…a work of argument…" Henri Bergson, Matter and Memory, trans. By Nancy Margaret Paul and W. Scott Palmer, NY: Zone Books, 1991, pp. 133-134).

I've got to admit it, as I tell myself my story, I feel as if I were embedded in myself, appreciating, in an article sent back to the States, happier moments with soldiers playing baseball or eating burgers in the PX. Or else a disagreable, gory, disastrous, sickening, ulcerous 15,000 wounded men covered with vomit and unavoidable urine, all that scrambled out, censored. I write about U.S. soldiers as if they were on long term furloughs, or else getting bullet-proof vests from their mothers back home in and that, under cover of anonymity, otherwise Rumsfeld would have been humiliated. I could just have written about those soldiers, amputated of arms and legs and forever living a disastrous life in a military hospital far away from the possibility of a periodic visit from their parents. Or those shipped back in simple wooden boxes Jews prefer when buried in a cemetery.

Imagine how my faithful readers would react to such glum news or, for that matter, my managing editor, if not the people in Washington and especially the occupier of the White House, now perhaps rebaptized the Black House, were I to write in a so-called foreign language so close to Derrida's analyses of Joyce's Finnigans Wake or Lacan's equally revealing Dupin's abilities, questionably translated by Baudelaire?

I once believed anyone could read and write. I've now changed my mind, having taught for the last sixty years. I'm assured that reading Bataille's Madame Edwarda or Francis Ponge's La rage de l'expression is nearly impossible even though the SAT scores have considerably risen over the past few years ("No child left way behind.") I especially appreciate Ponge's "La Mounine" or his "Mimosa" where, after having provided the reader with his ecstatic rapport with that flower in the brief first section, went over to the Littré (OED for you) and lifted words to put directly in the poem as well as analyzing all the linguistic puns in the title of the poem. (You're getting too much! Get back to Southampton.) A last word at least for the moment: Kant's meaning "fullness" without any specific meaning. Such is Southhampton, torn between wealth and wealth approachable; if you turn left on Job's Lane, there's the Parrish Art Museum and to the right, J. McLaughlin's haberdashery store. Then the light, left again onto Main Street, a little further down Main, you turn left again and enter the parking lot, not far from Hildrith's department store where once I tried to buy a beach chair only to be told that they were out of it. "You know, the season…" I could have purchased deck chairs, rattan furniture, glass tables for the patio, a teak table, and hammocks of all colors as well, as well as large parasols, presuming the guests at table were so numerous that such would have been the need. The salesman, courteous, eyeing perhaps a commission, quick to answer my questions, once again said "If you need anything, please call."

Outside the store, at paced intervals, wooden benches where old and not so old sat, looking at cars passing by: brand new red Jaguars, an elegant 1938 Mercedes (a collector's item. Did Hitler ride in one of them?) MG's, hugging the ground (what would they have done in a Mexican electrical thunder storm instantaneously transforming Main Street into a river?) and a gorgeous white convertible Rolls Royce, no doubt slumming in Southampton, and owned by someone living off some discreet side street in East Hampton in a totally renovated mansion with an Olympic size pool, a pool house and lots and lots of deck chairs heavily cushioned, and all doors electrically wired to reduce the pressure of the hand when opening any door. Smithson, speaking about his sublime Spiral Jetty wrote "the alogos undermines the logos" (Quoted in Arthur Danto's review in the "Nation," September 19, 2005, p. 34). Saw mulled old couples sitting on those benches. There they are until they become "were." On the corner of Main and Nugent Saks Fifth Avenue. If you were logical, what's this "Fifth Avenue" doing on that corner? I never went in but I did eat soup in a paper cup across the street. I walked back and saw a sedate man's store; the window had a radiant jacket with elbow patches, tweedy looking slacks and matching ties and belts. Beyond my means. I prefer an adventure, entering a resale shop, only open Thursdays, Fridays and Saturdays. Upstairs, in the men's section, five handsome shirts, collars all 17 ½, no doubt having belonged to one neck. Brooks Bros, Valentino, Prada and an assortment of double-breasted blazers with colored slacks right for beach parties. Downstairs, a kind lady, who takes your cash, answers questions. If only she had had a Patek Philippe bought recently at Tourneau's and sold by some impecunious bus driver to whom the watch had been given as a Christmas gift! The other watches, under glass, were all, all of them, preposterous in size or in the eye-blinding numbers usually the 12, much larger than other numbers. As Charles Quint expressed it: "Il faut être propriétaire d'une belle montre pour être Maître de soi-même. »

What's left of Southhampton (practically all for sale, and perhaps it will turn out to be another Westhampton with a great number of Real Estate Agencies and banks)? A melancholy retrospective when they entertained Black Panther readers of Fanon's The Wretched of the Earth, (recently retranslated by

Richard Philcox), all that, either in Suffolk County or on Park Avenue below 80th street.

Now onto the Richest Ladies of the Southampton Club (RLSC) who invited every other month a celebrity from Paris to speak in French since all those ladies had spent their Junior Year in Paris, going to the Spring Fashion Show and buying out the whole Dior collection. The hardy ones flew over to Milan to check out the runway. But to banish their inferiority complex, they always found a speaker and this time Turgot who was to talk about his latest work: Réflexions sur la formation et la distribution des richesses. The ladies were delighted. Wasn't it more intellectually satisfying than sitting behind a make-shift table and selling used clothing to benefit the Cancer Research Foundation?

Turgot was equally delighted. His A-R (round trip) was payed for and he received a modest honorarium of $10,000.

I believe Rousseau was right in his portraiture of contemporary society wherein he traced physical inequalities having given way to an economic system of inequalities (See the Second Discourse, part two). Rousseau went as far as hyperbolizing the "poor" as the "starving people" ("Affamés"). He further developed his negative judgement of society as that world where the rich were protected by the law and not the poor.

Power defined class and wealth defined class. When the decrepits sat on those wooden benches, saw conspicuous consumption, people leaving elegant stores, holding elegant bags with the handsome gold-lettered name of the store, they knew. And they also knew how to tell one class from another just by looking at women passing by, overloaded with diamond rings, another one in both ears, perhaps even one around the ankle ("nouveau riche"). For them, aging was of no concern. They wintered in their West Indies homes, swam in blue waters, sunbathed half undressed. Italian bathing suits. Their creepingly marked faces and their arms, all of a sudden, were lined with insistant folds, botoxed in the fall; a seasonal habit saved by a diagnosis indicating the beginning of skin cancer and then that skin had to be removed leaving—for a moment—a harsh sign of a surgical intervention. Acupuncture at home by an elderly Chinese specialist, heat treatments, massages on their own folded tables by a Swedish masseuse and frequent swims in a 15 x 15 heated pool, represented the latest in rejuvenation. They ate melba toasts, lots of yogurt ("zéro matière grasse"), cottage cheese; no fruits, no French baguettes, no cheeses, no "saucisson d'Arles" (you fill in the rest of their delicious Spartan menus...)

I see them slowly walking with their white poodles, held often enough as they caress their fur and sometimes, inadvertently of course, encouraging a minor erection. No matter. Among Southhampton ladies, everything is justified and no need to justify anything, in the name of Saks on the corner and open-ended accounts.

Sometimes she feared the day when, on the sly, purchasing a sable at a 57th Street resale shoppe, someone might recognize her among those hurried West Side elderly ladies jumping on hand-me-down furs.

She did have a marked if secretive advantage. While in the fall, all of her girlfriends dressed to attend a 17th century French drawing exhibit at Wildenstein's, she would sneak out, wearing her 1958 Chanel blue suit, take business class on Air France (Ah! Those were the days...) and spend a couple of weeks seeing her Parisian friend, a descendant of the comtesse de Ségur. She lived in a duplex pentouse facing what once had been Louis Philippe's royal residence, later state-seized and turned into the elegant Parc Monceau where both of them, early morning risers, jogged. They often encountered well-dressed children attending the Ecole Active Bilingue, facing one of her preferred museums: Cernuschi. At other times she would go up North to visit another of her favorite museum: Gustave Moreau and his splendid decadent paintings.

Once a week, both of them, with two other friends, would

go slumming. She remembered (but it wasn't that long ago...) Thursday teas on the first floor of the Café Flore. On Fridays, upscaled, they had tea in the Hotel Raphaël lounge.

The descendant, nevertheless, on Sunday mornings, ensconced in her silk sheets, read last year's Prix Goncourt, to assure her of something to say on Thursdays and Fridays.

Southhampton, I believe, suffers from an inferiority complex. East Hampton has a huge synagogue and a once a year baseball game where all the players are the local big names: writers, poets, artists, etc., etc. Dear Southhampton is bereft of both. However (and that's a big however!) in order to justify themselves and their hard-earned station, having managed to go Beyond Good and Evil, and they quoted that well-known philosopher, here worth noting: "a keen and far-reaching analysis...touching upon various influences of Christianity." I'll stop here for a moment.

It is bruited about that women who go to schul on Friday nights are essentially there to find a match or outmatch another lady's outfit. Thus those preposterous hats, overshadowing their eyes, making them look like a Taliban female in a future burkha. Or their diamond studded high heels, their extremely expensive suits (no blouses or skirts), a sign of an august event.

What they know with fervor is "the relation between religious ecstasy and sensuality...Indeed a negation of will." (Nietzsche)

All those strolling women either single, married or widowed! Let me open another sexy digression. Question: "why are single women single and what explains their enthusiastic religious devotion?"

In the first instance, a streak of an outright lesbian rejection of coupling with the other sex; a profound but unabashed definition of selves and their troubling sexuality, relieved by a well-placed finger. This leads to a coupling when, in front of a large mirror, they begin to fondle each other, kissing mouths and ending up using one of Sonia Reykiel's blue-colored dildos, especially made for women ashamed of buying such tools of pleasure in the Clichy neighborhood. "Instincts and desires, partially and provisionally defined." (See philosopher named above.)

To admit to one's declared longing, momentarily negating one's own will in order to allow the body's penchant (as the marquis de Sade stipulated) is a natural urge and a revelation "avoiding the real problem...dominated by class..."

But all had read Nietzsche's "Preface" to his mastering piece and I quote from Helen Zimmern's translation (NY: The Modern Library, 1927, p. 377): "Supposing that Truth is a woman..." Let's take that seriously and suppose that Truth cleans up some darkened areas because we too equate Truth with women, capable "perhaps," as the author stipulates, to "play upon words..." (Remember Nietzsche was initially a linguist and those who translate him are forced into lengthy explanatory footnotes).

Thus women express Truth but in such a way as to force the common reader into a distasteful situation or an avowed ignorance or, on the contrary, equating Truth with irreverent puns understood only by "the happy few." Theirs is a Dyonesian propensity, however well-kept in a secret closet of the body. A hazardous psycho-psychological condition.

The other woman, equally defined by her equation with Truth, with a Truth and synagogal events, searches for a husband or a lover. In each case wishing for Oedipus to relieve her—later on— of a cumbersome husband. The crossroad, where the inaugural deed was done, was marked by Saks on one side, the soup place on the other.

As a consequence, out of this manicured desire (it's all in the eye and that's hard to define: odor di femina of the highest perfume). But "the fakeness of an opinion is not for us an objection." (Truth in language).

Maliciously, such unmarried women weave their web of charm on an unwitting male, having first ascertained his visible signs of wealth, a ruby on his pinky, a discreet diamond earring, depending on his age. Ferragamo tasseled loafers and a cashmere ribbed sweater around his neck in spring and autumn and worn regularly in winter, but on special occasions, let's say a late Sunday brunch. If young admissible, if old, vulgar.

They may know the Truth of a perfect future match but does the opposite sex know as much? And so begins a slow mating dance, however muted, however apparently passive-aggressive. As beasts in a cage put there for procreating purposes, man and woman smell each other, appreciate, on the one hand, cups of breasts (not too enormous…) and, not too heavy a penis, pushing through well-selected slacks. That particular interest- penis in flight- if overly significant, is sought after, mimicked by muffled cries of passion. She already imagines her first date, going dancing at the French Kiss. She dreams of her left arm going around his neck, pressing and wiggling against his body, while his hand deftly moves south until he clutches her ass, little knowing that right there, she has herpes blotches, sometimes recused into a blemish under a doctor's prescription. He saw with pleasure a dimple on her left cheek, close to her nostril. She never knew, but he had a herniated disc.

She: I love Anaïs Nin.
He: I love Ian Hugo.
She: both of us like art, don't we?
He: I love you.
She: I love you, too.
A third voice: Have a…good day!

I follow her eyes as they broadly verify if "he" is a rich catch much like fishermen off Montauk hoisting up a 200 pound tuna. And if he is worthy of her desires, if his family is well connected, owns a town house off Gramercy Park and an old and respected mansion out of Southhampton? Furthermore, if they have a personal trainer come to both their abodes, if they "spa" in winter, if they have subscriptions to the Met, the old Yankee stadium, the Joyce and membership in the NYAC.

If her anxious wishes were only corporal! The marquis de

Sade made a good case for that. But she slowly wonders if the pills she has been religiously wallowing to tame her overt sexual drives, were matched by the viagraed male she has, for better or for worse, selected.

"Ah!" she exclaims to herself: "isn't one pill equal to another?" Or, she wonders fearfully, could he, a bi-polar in need, periodically desert her, deprive her of her allowance or straight away (as the Brits say) beat her up?

It's fine to catch a young man recently out of Harvard's Business School or was it the Jewish Theological Seminary? But doubts afflict her, haunt her body's heat. It might be a wiser choice (as Juliette once muttered to herself) to pick an aging millionaire, stiff with investments, yet keen on possessing a young woman to walk his Great Dane. In his own way he listened to a different music and, after all, who would walk his dog? Others might consider this a tragicomedy. In reality, it was his hedge fund. In his choice he'd rather spend his last years in a retirement community, protected by guards and an electric fence not far from an 18 hole golf course. In fact, the millionaire says to himself: "before death arrives in a dark windowed limousine to carry him off to an expensive family vault, reserved for the likes of him, why, indeed, not get married?"

Furthermore, just to convince him of the rectitude of possible sexual escapades, he summoned up his college escapades. Now, with retrospective wonder, he remembers (summons up) the first virgin he deflowered, Mary Jane (Hans Bellmer photographed her in the late forties shoes accompanied by ankle socks and tied to a tree) in a mini skirt revealing, when she sat down, provocatively, her see-through underwear, offered to any sight seer. How they panted, or made believe, and alluding to a priestly lexicon, how they fornicated. An inaugural experience for both. But he flooded her, excitedly jerking just to make it last longer. Both lit a cigarette afterwards and talked about the forthcoming basketball game. "Would you date me for the game?" She answers "I'll have to check my appointment calendar and I'll let you know. Don't call me. I'll call you." A few hours later, she accepted on his recording machine (one of the very first to have been put on the market). Then she added: "Pick me up in front of my sorority," which he did with alacrity, hoping to repeat last night's prowess. In his red Porsche convertible, top down, of course, he turned his thoughts to the bushes behind the sorority with hopes of doing it again but, as in Marguerite Duras's instance, allowing all the young women to gawk at them from all of the windows.

His older brother, back from Vietnam, told him about smoking endless pot, fucking ugly prostitutes, saved by a flag put over their heads and he laughed: "Fuck for Old Glory!"

How much he would have preferred Betty Grable or Rita Hayworth!

As he mused about his college days, he also remembered why he had chosen Southhampton for his secondary residence. In fact, everything had been decided long before when, his friend, wishing to celebrate his 25th birthday, invited him to his grandiose property out of town. The minute I got there, I said to myself, this is the place I want to live in. A day after his own birthday, he started playing the stock market, checking in mid-afternoon on CNN how the Dow was doing, the Nasdaque, S&P, PBC, RWA, QVQ and foreign markets as well. His investments grew, prospered. His bank accounts spiraled upwards as did returns on his savings (a cautious man). Soon he had enough money to go to a Westhampton Real Estate Agency off Main Street. He settled on a dream house in Southhampton for 5 million dollars, readily available, thus no bank loans, cash on the barrel, in a large valise. Before moving in, he had the whole house gutted, put in new bathrooms (five of them) a brand new kitchen (it reminded him of a Jacques Tati film) as well as a twenty seat screening room in the refurbished basement. To congratulate himself on a job well done, he bought an Etruscan vase and Egyptian medallion he had made into a ring, sure that nobody else in Southhampton had one. His project was to attend an opening at the East Hampton Guild Hall wearing his new acquisition, a $39,700 Lange and Söhn, Grand Langermatik watch. He would attend, with a telling delay, wearing a red T-shirt from Cacharel. Arms bare, of course...

Now, a great many years later, he eyed that young woman eyeing him from across the room (a song he once had heard). "Would you care to join me in a ride in my white convertible RR?" It didn't take her long to drop the Porsche for a more substantial vehicule.

BACK IN PARIS

An e-mail from Fred to Adam at the NYT: "Should I follow up on this lead and check out Gavronsky's interest in beauty?"

Adam to Fred: "Do it. But make it readable."

Once again Fred ran to the locker and found the names of Gavronsky's cousins. He talked to his new-found friends at Reid Hall, rue de Chevreuse.

He managed to locate the three cousins plus François Dominique, his co-translator of Louis Zukofsky's epic poem, "A," living on rue de Velars, Plombières-les-Dijon. There, at the local boulangerie, talking to the taciturn lady while her husband read his newpaper, he picked up a mustard Chicken recipe. He found another friend who knew Gavronsky and who lived next to a small vineyard in Montmartre.

Gavronsky, in Kant's footsteps, was struck by the apparent incompatibility of two species of common sense. He discovered what he was later to coin as an "Antinomy of Taste." Should I decipher this for his obit or just leave it as is?

Well, if it's a question of taste, and Gavronsky's cautious and contentious surrounding of the above formula, it was momentarily evident (as Descartes proposed) that this antinomic categorization, allowing the co-existence of an antithesis, could well work itself into his own schema of things. In that way, so he thought, he would get away with murder, playing Zero Mostel singing "On the one hand..."

Fred mused. What were the signs or signals sent out by Gavronsky when he looked at a painting, like Caravaggio's "Judith Beheading Holofernes?"

He wrote in his notebook that that painting was Caravaggio's first truly dramatic subject. Gavronsky appreciated the velocity of horror, the nearly impossible task of a writer to translate into words the move from youthful paintings to this naturalistic vision, actually nearly impossible to look at, so bloody, so gory.

It certainly had nothing to do with Clement Greenberg's insistence on purity in painting. Why, in Caravaggio's time, should horror elate a sense of beauty? Would we have said that Jackson Pollock's work was purer and thus more beautiful?

Such "recherché" postulates may, so he wrote, avoid reading a painting, the one which inspired a poem and yet...he remembered Derrida's analysis of Van Gogh's peasant boots so different from Heidegger's or Meyer Shapiro's. Where then is Beauty and why bring in extra painterly commentaries as if those boots were insufficient onto themselves or the shoe laces for that matter? Fred wrote in his notebook: "Get back to the question of poetry at a later time." Here it is, the topos of a beheading and its impact on the viewer seeking a vision of Beauty of the whole. A gestalt approach. Gavronsky also commented on John Ashbery's Portrait in a Convex Mirror in an article which appeared in Speculum, dealing with Francisco Parmigianino's painting of the same title. Gavronsky wrote: "the beauty is in the mirror, in the speculation, its sexual inferences, the richness of its intertextual references. In an instant, he wrote, "I know what it does and does not know; this allows me to dream, to construct my own painting, much as Ashbery had done. Looking inside a mirror is something like Cocteau's mirror through which we enter into another world. Part of the charm (etymologically speaking) is the Leonardesque sfumato and that beckoning hand playing with the viewer, riveted by the mirror, its convexity, as a sign of femininity. In latin, Speculum means mirror as it suggests an instrument used by a doctor to check a woman's body."

He wrote: "Have you ever read John Rideval's description of the image of the prostitute—blond, mutilated ears and a proclaimed strumpet (a criminal). "She also had a deformed face which was obviously full of diseases. There, word for word, word after word, in fact a chain of words all tending to represent a painting.

Sit in an art history class, watch 50 slides in 50 minutes, hear a word for each painting, let's say, "look at his panama hat" or "check out where his eyes are going…" or again, "Appreciate the religious interferences in Titian's Allegory of the Three Parts of Prudence."

Sitting there in the dark facing "Beauty," this time in quotes, you wonder if, besides being remarkably beautiful and crowned, this lady…And added here more descriptive words, a mini-narration doubling the painting, or perhaps a "screening" of one's own memories going back to graduate school?

A sign in your notebook, allowing you to bone up for the final exam. "Professor, could you give us a hint as to what we can expect on the final?" "I expect you to identify 15 of the thirty slides and for 10 of them, provide me with as complete an analysis as possible." He added, "furthermore, I'm only interested in you defining Beauty."

3 years later, now in a mid-Western Junior College, with a powerpoint, he repeated: "John Rideval's appreciation of this painting is a classic. Question: "Why do you think he was so taken by that painting?"

3 years later, it became the hallmark of his presentations. "Should I go over what I've just described?" He took off his glasses, folded his notes and left the room before the bell rang.

There may be another discourse. Derrida: the frame—"le passe-partout," the title, signature, where it hung in a museum, archives, previous owner(s), encouraging a philosophical « detour » : judging art as a « pararegon, » a supplement, what is left, what has been sidelined, what manner of approaching it...And thus his own sun. Does that explain Derrida's Louvre exhibit which he curated from January 21 1990 to 1991, entitled "Memories of the Blind: Autoportraiture and other Ruins." And he followed (eyes wide open...) a number of paintings where blindness existed and, for example, Annibale Carrachi's Polyphemus, eyes that kill, those of the Gorgone's eyes pierced, Oedipus, the Cyclop...

At least an ambitious philosophical recounting of the word-work. Perhaps the word preceeding the dancer's arm, the musician's note, the painter's brush or the writer's hand...Is there a way of circumscribing language? It depends on the "pararegon" application, the detail in the word (check out Roland Barthes' S/Z,) a dismemberment of the alphabet.

The bell always rings at this crucial moment. Was the voice preceeded by its shadow?

Somebody asked: "what about Santiago Calatrava's sculpture before the actuality of beauty? His multiform, honey-combed elongated rental tower in Malmö or an engineer's thought? A move, a translation, a language exhibited out of man's talents..."

As a young Japanese journalist, working for the "Asahi Shimbun" or was it the "Mainichi Shibun"? insisted in Arakawa's and Madeline Gins's flat, in his Asiatic accent, that: "All is langage."

Hear the bells of Notre Dame de Paris or the ones in Chartres or Reims--does that sound, were it unheard, still exist? Would that be one of the possible definition of "Beauty?"

Lastly, at a book signing party at Rizzoli, a lawyer cum-art historian, when asked to define Beauty quickly answered "Culture." She knew, before she saw, that whatever was in front of her, her Italian Renaissance training had already always defined her vision.

Fred to Adam@NYTimes.Org.

"Hey, Adam! Should I follow up on Gavronsky's interest in beauty?"

Adam to Fred@reidhall.edu
"Do it but make sure it fits a three column obit."
Fred rummaged around in the locker. He talks to his newborn friends at Reid Hall; he manages to reach his three cousins. His co-translator and another one who knew him in Montmartre. Nothing worth noting.

THE JOURNALIST'S RECALL

I did not see the body lying in state in Sulzberger Parlor, Barnard Hall, third floor facing east, looking over Broadway to Columbia University. If you stood on the roof of Butler Hall you could see Harlem beneath your feet.

I did see photographs of Gavronsky on his bookshelf, as well as a number of "livres d'artistes" where he had handwritten his poetry and a painter (Italian, German, French...) had illustrated that hand-made "livre" and never more than in a limited edition of 6. There had also been printed works with an equal number of artistic interventions.

There, in the Parlor, a stream of friends and students passed by the bier, an object of adulation someone said, but another faculty member from Columbia corrected that view.

The now stilled body, soon to be disposed of, unlike Lenin's tomb, where, brushing away the horrors for which he had been responsible (a model for Stalin's later politics), all were, as they say, in their "heart of hearts" more or less convinced that, as the years passed by, so would his memory. In fact, 314 Milbank, his office, would be emptied of all books and paintings, the files thrown out of the two filing cabinets, a new paint job ordered (who would dispose of the books? That guy on 111th Street and Broadway, or some professional book-dealer called in for the job?) Someone else would take over the office. There wouldn't be a single trace left, indicating that here, in 314, Milbank, somebody had lived a good part of his life.

His present students, Kleenex in hand, wiping eyes and

cheeks, reverently passed through the double doors of the Parlor where, besides the handsome fireplace and a piano at the other extremity of the room, only chairs had been arranged, facing east, to allow speakers to vocalize their sentiments.

A former chairwoman of the Board of Trustees remembered him, as did a number of former colleagues who were also to die. As speakers spoke, heads nodded. "Don't you think it might be a beautiful idea to endow a chair in the French department honoring the memory of Serge Gavronsky and, let's say, at least a yearly invitation to a French poet?" Nobody jumped up, ready to hand over a million dollars for that chair.

DESCRIBING SOUTHHAMPTON (AGAIN)

A curious enterprise: In Suffolk County, ready like Levites from Ephraim who sent the body of his murdered wife, cut into twelve pieces, to spur the Tribes of Israel to revenge. In Riverhead, the body of Emma Bovary was sent—via FEDEX—to Southampton, for the town's millionaires to seek revenge on a stop of the LIRR where, factually, all of them, initially without cars, had to take the train, at times gawking at gays, always in perfect physical shape, getting off at Bayshore to take the ferry to Fire Island. Did those pieces, some looking exactly like Southampton matrons, stress the act or its effects? Or, as in a metaphor (see Aristotle's definition: "Metaphor is the transfer (epiphora) to a thing of a name that designates another thing..." Or a substitution. Here Emma's body (in pieces) would be more like an act. Once more a difference between symbolic and literal language. All this readiness, as in Rodin's self-sacrificing gentlemen of Calais, unable to free themselves in Southhampton from an on-going natural beach (private in most instances). Some might still consider this an antithesis or an unexpected digression breaking the narrative flow, considering the above etymological translation.

The gentlemen of Southhampton rejected all ideas of a common essence, even if there had been an initial agreement between the twelve parts packaged in a FEDEX package, even reconstructed piece by piece by the town's coroner. Henceforth, they proclaimed: "We shall never again sign for a FEDEX package." Or, would it be a perpetual hypothesis, frightening these millionaires, sleeping next to their wives or, worse, some of the older female graduates of their respective colleges met at an annual get-together? Or a Yale football game? Riverhead claimed it was all a practical joke. This bit of news truly put off our rich friends in town.

Truth, therefore, had been deprived of itself. How happy, really satisfied, if at least the language had persisted long after receiving that package! No. No more domination, no more Narcissus-like mirrored image of their anxious faces…Those fearful numbers cut out like unwilling testicles off a bull for some Chinese menu in Shanghai!

Is that part of the reason why Southampton has a grievous inferiority complex "à la" Jung ? Probably a bit further on the way to East Hampton and its resplendent synagogue, or its traditional baseball game, enlisting all the famous painters and writers in the immediate area (including Noyac, if you please, as well as Amagansett). "cher" Southampton, bereft of both.

However, in order to justify their hard-earned stations, having preceeded Beyond Good and Evil, they praised themselves for having attained the Nietzschean status : "a keen and far-reaching analysis…touching upon various influences of Christianity." And let me add Judaism. I'll stop here for a moment.

THE INTERVIEWER'S TAPE

There's nothing like an unexpected e-mail especially if it comes from the managing editor of your paper! Here's the heart of the matter (to quote a common expression): "Just received from SG's wife, a tape which might help you advance in your research."

Waidhofen an der Ybbs is a quiet 7000 citizen town. The Gymnasium faces the soccer field and, a little further back, the hospital, and I guess the cemetery behind the hospital. Anne-Marie was born there. Went skiing with her father in nearby mountains; rucksack on the back and tennis-like shoes that you put on when you were ready to slalom downhill. Her mother had died in an avalanche. Her father remarried an anti-Semitic monster, something I never suspected until I got there to propose. After I left to get back to Paris, she made her negatives known. "He's Jewish, isn't he?" Besides being an anti-Semite, she was more preoccupied with feeding her cat then taking care of her step-daughter whom she forced to bicycle to town, early in the morning, before classes began, to buy expensive liver for the cat.

When Anne-Marie was 17 she had her tonsils removed in a Viennese hospital. She then decided to leave her family house, garden and all, and live in Vienna where she had a slightly older cousin whose mother eventually decided to purchase the family house, just to be closer to her older and now married daughter. Then off to Italy and then to Cambridge to enroll in English for Foreigners, a language she quickly mastered.

In London, hired as a baby sitter, just to stay in that city, where she had arrived nearly penniless. There she was exploited by a distinguished British family with four children. "Take care of the laundry. Read the list I've prepared and go shopping around the corner. Do not dally and come back with the exact change. Do not forget to make the beds, feed the children breakfast, lùnch, and a "goûté" (she was pleased with the few words she had learned on a summer vacation in the Alps (not far from Courchevel) and then, after the after-school snack, vacuum the house." (They lived in a brownstone not far from the British Museum, though Anne-Marie never had an opportunity to see the Elgin Marbles, something she did with SG at a later date.

One day, Anne-Marie said without warning: "I quit."

"For your obit. Read this:"A Columbia College interviewer, specializing in faculty on both sides of Broadway, noted in a radio voice:

"You may be wondering why I invited you to WKCR, heard through the underground corridors all over campus. Well, as one of your Négritude students said recently, on this student-run program, you're a great teacher. We'll get back to that in a minute. Can you tell us about your undergraduate days at the college where you got a scholarship in 1950 that is, besides majoring in European History and studying German History with Fritz Stern. You also minored in French literature and took a number of courses with your adviser, Nathan Edelman, a specialist in 17th century French lit. I know he asked you, at the end of your sophomore year, "what do you want to major in?" You said, I believe, you hadn't yet made up your mind and he said, "great, you've got a whole year in front of you. I'll ask you the same question next year." By that time, Edelman supposed, I would have made up my mind. No! But I did accumulate enough courses to be a History major and a French minor (by the way, that's my mother's maiden name!)

SG. "First things first and that is, and always will be for me, working on WKCR with Peter Kennen, who later wrote John F. Kennedy's gold speech delivered in Berlin. Our program was called: 'Challenge of Power' and our faculty adviser was Professor Frankel, who was later murdered in his home in Bedford."

Interviewer: "What's this "Challenge of Power"?

SG: "Take for instance Luther's 96 theses pinned to the door of a cathedral. Correct me if I'm mistaken in the number of theses; after all, you're taking Contemporary Civilization! Then another challenge: The Terror played by that young and brilliant speaker and radical, Saint-Just and his older, sometimes referred to as a tyrant, Robespierre."

Interviewer: "How did you become vice president of Columbia Players?"

SG: "Great efforts do not necessarily jump start your extra-curricular career. In fact, as of my sophomore year, I auditioned for a part in "Billy Budd" and was given a small sailor's part on the deck of the old McMillan Theater. Then off to a great career as the First Tempter in T.S. Eliot's 'Murder in the Cathedral'."

FIRST TEMPTER
Your Lordship won't despise an old friend out of favour?
Old Tom, gay Tom, Becket of London,
And here a fifty cent piece the director had suggested I wind up in my black jogging pants to hold them up. It snapped snapped and landed on somebody's head in the audience!
"But the greatest lines were those of the Fourth Tempter."

FOURTH TEMPTER
You know and do not know, what it is to act or suffer.
You know and do not know that acting is suffering,
And suffering acting. Neither does the actor suffer
Nor the patient act...
How's that for a glorious piece of writing?

However, the most unexpected event was to follow. Off to Short Hills for another performance but, prior to our duties, the elderly ladies, enamored of T.S. Eliot, had prepared deviled eggs to satisfy what they assumed was our hunger after the bus ride from Manhattan. We did as we were told but the result was disastrous. In the middle of the play, Thomas a Beckett ran off stage to vomit in the wings. All of us followed suit but, heroically, we did manage to survive and the applause was uninterrupted by a diminishing audience (many of the ladies had to get to bed before 10 o'clock). When we performed in Baltimore, having been forewarned, nobody but nobody ate anything we were offered. Memorable souvenirs!

Maybe the best part of working on a set, rehearsing late into the night, were those three o'clock in the morning burgers at a now defunct restaurant near Shraffts.

And remember, Varsity shows in those days had no females. I once was dressed in a 'TUTU' and danced around the stage until some hefty football player lifted me up and twirled me around!"

Interviewer: "Tell us how you became interested in translation."

SG: "That's rather a long story, but for you, I'll be specific! Translation is a many-sided word. You can say, for example, that Thomas a Becket was translated from his cathedral to London. If you go to Athens, you'll see moving trucks with a big sign on the side: 'Metaphora.' In other words, moving something from here to there. That's quite close to Aristotle's definition. If I take myself as yet another Thomas a Becket, I moved from Paris to Lisbon and then, after an arduous trip, escaping Nazi subs, arrived in NY. I went to P.S. 54 on 107th street and there, Mrs. Lipman taught a huge class of foreign-born kids how to speak English. If you think about my granddaughter's class, the teacher has 29 students enrolled and we think that's outrageous! My only criticism, and that was during the war, she confiscated all our yo-yos made in Japan. How patriotic! But then we were all patriots. When the air raid alarm rang, all of us crouched beneath our desks! I went to the Nemo movie on 110th Street and Broadway where now Gristede's stands and saw Humphrey Bogart, Lauren Bacall and Peter Lorre, and a host of other great actors in "Casablanca." Just to show you how impressionable I was, I wept when they played the Marseillaise! At that time I joined the French Cub Scouts, and wore knickers which I pulled down as far as possible at times even reaching my ankles so that I wouldn't become the risible object of all looking at me! I was ashamed when I was whistled at in the subway going to South Ferry but there, in the Men's Room, all of us put on short pants and left NY for a hike on Staten Island. As of that moment, I hated Staten Island.

Mrs. Lipman in the spring smelled underarm garlic perspiration, but all of us, in that huge classroom, still loved her and she loved us, or so we believed. It didn't matter: we did learn English or rather, American.

I came to translation rather by accident, I mean "real"

translations when the great French poet, Francis Ponge, taught a whole semester's seminar at Barnard (Nathalie Sarraute couldn't come) on Lautréamont and Malherbe. He sat at the head of a long table in 306 Milbank. I caught him afterwards, and we took long walks down Amsterdam Avenue and then further downtown. He loved NY! My parents invited him for dinner where he spoke about his descendants, Henri IV, a solid Protestant. My father tried to veer the conversation away off toward Gogol or was it Chekhov? I don't remember. It didn't work.

In any case, as of that meeting, and many others, I decided to do a full-length book on contemporary French poets. Ponge, in his summer residence near Bar-Sur-Loup, where he had invited Anne-Marie and myself, suggested that the first question I should ask of all of 'my' poets was: 'Where do you place yourself within French literature?' He himself proudly answered his own query: "I am a branch off the tree of French literature." And off we went. If you want to read more of my questions and more of his answers, check out Poems and Texts, published by October House (in commemoration of the Russian Revolution).

I renamed my mini-anthology because Marcelin Pleynet insisted he would not be placed in an alphabetical work where Guillevic appeared (by that time Pleynet was no longer an active leftist). So Pleynet suggested Poems and Texts.

I'll never forget René Char's answer when I wrote him asking if he would be kind enough to talk with me, just to set up a different voice from those poems I had already translated.

"I never do an 'explication de texte!'" And that was that. (I should have asked Mary Ann Caws to intervene, but at that time I had no idea she knew Char). Some of the poets I did include had never been translated in English and, for example, Pleynet himself. A side note: Yves Bonnefoy came to my office, in the basement of Milbank. I asked him that consecrated question and, for the next forty minutes (I thought my tape would run out) he spoke of Gurjief. When he abruptly ended, he asked me to destroy the tape. In Paris he would mimick an oral style and answer all my hand-written questions. He also promised to provide me with a photograph of himself, an idea my publisher had suggested. Denis Roche had already been translated, but I'm not sure. André du Bouchet, who had gone to Harvard, thought his English better than mine until I told him 'English' wasn't the same as 'American'" (When a U.S. novel is translated in French, they always mention 'traduit de l'américain')."

INTERVIEWER'S STORY

"My name is Fred Smithson, my family's name is like that great American artist. I was born August 26, 1940. Because of my last name, that may be the reason, when later on, I always introduced myself as the "Other,' and laughed, since I could never, in a million years, tell anyone what Smithson actually did out there in the sand!

I look American, shave every day, and because of my frequent outdoor assignments, I've got a ruddy complexion, blue-grey eyes, as my passport indicates. I weigh 155 lbs but I haven't always weighed that much!

As a young kid, living in Nassau County, I skipped around a lot. Mom and father, as of that moment, cut out the 'Fred' and went for 'Skip.'" I'm still with that monicker when I go see my parents in Dallas where my folks moved into a middle class retirement home. Mom says she hates it because she doesn't play bridge or canasta. Father loves it because he's pretty good on that 18 hole golf course. Besides, it gives him a chance to shmooze with other elderly gentlemen! There's a full-time-doctor on the premises as well as a nurse from St. Kitts. Nobody talks about them; and besides, the hospital is a couple of miles down the road. There's also a cemetery. The brochure doesn't mention it. Besides, if anything were to happen to mom or father, I'd have to fly back to Dallas, and especially now that I'm on assignment in Paris doing research on SG for my now extended obit, it would be difficult.

As you may know, SG has been teaching at Barnard ever since 1961, first as a part-time instructor (making $5000.00 a year) and later as a full-time member of the French department. (I found out how he got his first job. His mother knew Professor Pleasants at Columbia where she was the resident linguist. She called her one day and told her the French department urgently needed someone to teach a class. It appears that unexpectedly enrollments had jumped up in the first half of 'Masterpieces of French Literature'" (FR BC 21). He was briefly interviewed by the chair, Professor Le Roy C. Breunig and hired on the spot. SG's French was impeccable and that was the real reason for the hire."

SG asked the first question: "what is the first reading?"

Answer: "Tristan et Iseut."

SG: "I never read the book."

Answer: "Read the episode on the sword in Curtius' study."

I did. That was fine for the fall semester.

I broke my back preparing, reading and writing out my class notes. Early on, a student asked me why all those notes? "I'm new here!" That same student then went on about her English professor who sat on the edge of his desk and said: "Isn't Milton's sonnet beautiful?" All those dutiful English majors, who hoped to become professors themselves, took down that divine statement, and you could hear them on their first job, discussing Milton's sonnet and, out loud, saying "isn't it beautiful?"

Then, a slightly older student, she may have been in her 20's, came to my office, wishing to discuss Tristan a bit further. A while later, I got a phone call from her businessman father: "My daughter truly enjoys your company, discussing French literature. I'm paying a weekly hour with her psychiatrist and all she does is discuss French literature. Would you like to take over? I'd pay you the same for the hour?"

I shriveled. "Sorry," I replied and saying that, hung up.

After her graduation, she got a job at Partisan Review. She

called a while later inviting me to a PR party. I was married. She never called again. I guess she hadn't read enough French literature!

SG wrote three novels (excluding this one). Apart from novels, he also wrote a great deal of French poetry and a considerable number in English: one book of poetry in English and seven in French.

At his death, he was waiting for a British publisher to give him the OK on his last book of poetry: "ANDORTHE."

So "Skip" finished high school. The building is now a condo but then, in the stairwell, he used to feel up those willing females…enough to get his morale up and pass the SAT's.

That fall semester he enrolled as a freshman at Harvard.

He wore a blue blazer, button-down Brooks Bros shirts, khaki slacks and loafers like everybody else.

Grades then were less important than who was your father, what was his annual income, what were his clubs and professional associations and, if he was white and not Jewish…

I majored in English with a minor in French. My very first instructor never got his tenure. He either switched careers and went into law or was hired by some little-known mid-western junior college. He had been quite brilliant at Columbia College where he had had the joy of being in one of Professor Lionel Trilling's classes. What luck for Trilling even though the then president of the university had supposedly indicated to the English department: "You've got your Jew, now keep it at that."

Inspired by that teacher (who smoked filtered cigarettes which, in a debonair fashion, he held in his left hand; the right hand playing with his glasses.) In his teaching he had one course, "Class and Self" where we read: Hard Times, Emma, D. H. Lawrence's short story, "Rocking Horse Winner" and, I almost forget, Orwell's Hommage to Catalonia and D. H. Lawrence's Lady Chatterly's Lover. I bought my novels at the corner bookstore now no more (now it's a Chinese restaurant). There, all by myself, I discovered

Tropic of Cancer, the marquis de Sade's Les infortunes de la vertu and Rousseau's Discourse on the Origin and Foundation of Inequality.

After graduation, near the top of my class, I got into Columbia's graduate program in English.

What did I do during all those years? Well, I spent as much time as possible seeing movies on 42nd Street. I also went to MOMA to pick up art students. I really thought I knew how to write when I transposed Godard's filmic theories into my prose. I did that instead of photographing reality which, viewing society, seemed to me to be characteristic of American novels: realism at all cost and what a bore. I especially appreciated Derrida's analysis of Edmond Jabès's work.

I drank beer at the West End.

Ginsberg wrote Latin verses.

I spent late nights somewhere else, probably at McSorley's in the Village.

My greatest literary influence was Desnos's La Liberté ou l'Amour. There I discovered a new way of structuring a novel in a fragmented manner where individuals appear and disappear, where Desnos duplicates some of de Sade's scenes. Bunuel was to do the same in "L' âge d'or."

I had nowhere else to go.

I met Sophie (Rousseau's L'Emile). I hated social dancing. I wasn't any good as a social drinker, and I really had very little to say about contemporary American poets.

In priestly lexicon, we fornicated in her flat off Central Park, with a window overlooking the reservoir. For me and for Sophie as well, all of that was a pastime.

One day I found an ad: "Looking for a young man able to read and write decent English." I went to the 45th floor of a lawyer's bld. Hired. I began by photocopying briefs, the most boring type of work. Clearly, I wasn't cut out for such a fascinating task.

By chance I bumped into the managing editor of the City

Desk at the "Times." A fabulous chance meeting. We quickly got along, reminiscing about our undergraduate days at Harvard. We had taken some of the same classes.

He quoted Spinoza: "The human body can be affected in many ways, whereby its power of activity is increased or diminished..." Or again, "Human infirmity in moderating and checking the emotions I name bondage." Both statements seemed to apply in one way or another to our human condition. I stopped playing tennis in Central Park and immediately started at the City Desk as a "murder specialist." Off to the Bronx, back to the Bronx, now Flatbush, now Avenue C between 10th and 11th street. The body was still warm when I arrived. After a while, getting up my courage, I asked the manager if there wasn't something else I could do. He said:"Obits," and ever since, that's where I've been, with my own desk and now my own secretary. So many people die every day and if most of them were anonymous, poor bastards, others were illustrious and that made my day. Now it's SG I'm researching, but in a way, it's beginning to read like my first novel! So here I am in Paris, checking out as many sources as possible.

I almost forget something amusing. At a Barnard graduation, where I found myself for a niece's good job over four years of work, I accidentally shook SG's hand since his daughter was also graduating that afternoon. We sat on the lawn.

The graduating class sat in front of us. We looked toward the Library doors. They had put up a red carpet on the platform with the proper dignitaries sitting there, and a guest speaker ready to utter words of wisdom.

JOLTED MEMORIES

Somehow, I knew it would come through the mail.

"Your local draft board wishes to see you on Thursday, March 21st, twelfth floor, room 1222."

The guard asked for my ID. I showed him my "Times' photograph. It didn't impress him one bit, but he did let me go up.

"You can go in now, Mr. Gavronsky." I did what I was told. Knocked on the double oldish looking wooden doors. Entered.

"Mr. Gavronsky, take a seat."

Outside, it began to rain. Dirty puddles and then bigger ones. People tried to get around them or jump over them. The grate on the corner was covered over by dead leaves. The water accumulated on the corner and then spread out, following the gutter's path. Crowds of secretaries, just returned from lunch, held their high heels in hand and tried to avoid getting really wet. It was now raining hard. I could hear it on the window of the room I was in. Feet drenched, the bottom of each dress hung like some miserable piece of clothing, washed and hung from a rope in the backyard of a Staten Island house. Some of the secretaries's underwear shown through their wet dresses, somewhat like a cheap Hollywood movie or "Bitter Rice."

"Mr. Gavronsky, do you mind?"

I sat stolidly looking at my "neighbors" though I didn't recognize any of them. The principal one, weighing over 250 lbs, light brown hair, probably 6'2," wore a loose fitting jacket, trousers which, clearly, hadn't been pressed in a long time and a pair of white socks inside cheap shoes. The white socks reminded me of those day laborers visiting friends or family on Sunday for a late breakfast.

Question: "How far are you in your studies, Mr. Gavronsky, now that you've received two deferments?"

Answer: "Almost finished with the last draft of my Ph.D dissertation."

Question: "Once that's over with, I suspect you'll go for your doctorate?"

I nearly laughed my head off! But decided that wasn't the right moment.

Question: "I see you've studied French. They'll probably send you to Okinawa (and he laughed inside his sleeve). You'll love it there; good food, ample broads and not too far from Japan and there, wow, what a time you'll have!"

"You may go now. You'll soon be getting a letter from the Army as to where you'll report for the mental and physical exams. Hope you pass them," said the fat one.

Leaving, I said to myself: "Fuck you all, dear neighbors."

Two weeks later, downtown at the induction center. First yell. "Get your asses ready for your physical."

"Get on your knees," a dictatorial doctor said. He then put on a rubber glove and stuck it up our asses, repeatedly saying: "No prostate, no obvious signs of cancer." Then he systematically pushed two fingers up our scrotum."Cough!"

All of us were told to strip and wait in the next room. A terrible stench. Without anybody making any signals, all of a sudden a guy got on the only chair, waved his right arm, and began perorating:

"And say, To-morrow is Saint Crispian;
This story shall good soldier teach his son
And Crispin Crispian shall n'er go by,
From this day to the end of the world,
We few, we happy few, we band of brothers
That fought with us upon Saint Crispin's day."

Instantanous applause, especially from the people who, in 10th grade, had done their Shakespeare.

Herded into the next room, we were told to get ready for an arduous exam. We dutifully sat down on beaten-up wooden desks. The test was handed out as were small pencils. "Put YES if you agree or NO if you don't, then hand me the test. I'll be sitting in front of you all, so no cheating. There's some space for you to write down something more personal."

My buddy had told me that, if I wanted to get out of the service, all I had to do was answer in the most compromising manner and for instance (I did precisely as he had told me to do) write down: "First sarge I see, I'll kill him." Or again, "I piss in bed" or again "I love boys" or finally, "If I'm drafted, I'll never speak again."

Outside, the rain stopped. Puddles dried out by the sun. The secretaries, humidified by their walk in the rain, were now getting out of the subway, running to their respective food stores. Some took out Chinese; others Indian and some even got hungry for sushi. One religious Jew hit the kosher deli and asked for a take-out pastrami sandwich.

My turn had yet to come. Dr. G. Stein, having been told about my answers, had me called to his closet. Of Austrian background, actually trained by Anna Freud, he had a wicked accent which I really can't imitate. Here, you're on your own.

"Pleeze sits down."

I did as I was told.

He began in earnest. "Rrroll up your zleeve," checking out if I had needle marks. "Do you like your perentz?" "Sometimes I do, sometimes I don't."

"Your fadder? Do you geztt along mit hym?" "Sometimes I do, sometimes I don't."

"Vat about goils?" "Sometimes I do, sometimes I don't."

The doctor got up and wrote down, in perfect English, "Highly aggressive but acceptable for military duty." (I later read that succinct report.)

Next stop Fort Dix. Green uniforms. Crew cuts.

The sarge yells out: "If you guys do anything out of order, you'll give me fifty." He meant fifty push ups with a rifle on your back, just to add to our breathing pain.

The next morning, at 6 o'clock, into the field for our first bayonet practice.

"See those straw men in front of you? Put your bayonets straight out and yell Kill, Kill, Kill and lunge at them. Remember, one of those straw guys might be a Jap stomach."

Undergraduates, citing SG's translation of Joyce Mansour's poetry, raised their voices in unison:

Let me love you.

I love the taste of your thick blood
I savor it in my toothless mouth. I love your sweat

. . ...

Let me lick your closed eyes
Let me pierce them with my pointed tongue.
You can imagine the sergeant's reaction. "Gimme me 75. And no fuckin around."
Not to be outdone in their literary tastes, all these college graduates, quoting Carl Sesar's translations of Catullus, went all the way with XXXII.

Amabo, mea dulcis Ipsithilla...
And the translation:
Come on, my little Ipsithilla, sweet,
You delicious piece, be a good girl
....
Nouem continuas fututiones
And spread out nine straight fucks for me

Now the sarge, with a squeegee head, turned to all of us. "Quite a piece of ass, Catullus had! Not bad for college graduates, but still, to keep up analogies, gimme fifty right now and be sure to kiss the grass when you do." His English had remarkably improved. It must have been the combo between Latin and English.

Every morning, when the trumpet sounded and the flag climbed up the pole, we had to rise and shine, make our beds, just the way we were taught, slip the sheet in a triangle under the mattress, and make sure our foot lockers were impeccably ready for inspection. We neither yelled out another poem nor fail to do exactly as we had been told. The captain comes in. Lifts up a blanket. "Okay," he says. Opens up a foot locker and "hey, soldier, be a bit more attentive and don't give me that shit about going to sleep too late."

Disgusting breakfast, shit on a shingle and coffee brewed during the Wang Jin I dynasty.

Now the ritual. The Sarge takes us out to a speck of lawn. "All I wanna see are asses and elbows." We picked up every butt, every chewing gum wrapper and god know what else.

That night, not quite out of despair, still strong enough to turn pages, I began reading, for distraction purposes, John Heartfield (1891-1968). "You must remember that he changed the relationship between art, politics and photography during a time when it seemed impossible to defeat the ferocious propaganda campaign proposed and implemented by evangelical Christians, all in favor of President G. W. Buisson and his unquenchable thirst for a good-looking victory in Irak." I envisaged two distinct planets. One up there, the other down here, with all of us, or nearly all of us. We began reciting "à haute voix" an unexpected litany listed below, and you may or may not wish to read it. In that case, skip to the following recollections of military duty.

All wheel-drive callipers
Allen wrenchcamshaft
Alternator caster
Automatic transmission cetane rating
Axle chassis
Ball joint clutch
Biocidecoil spring
Blow-up cooling recovery system
Bushing cranking
Nifty, isn't it?

After that grueling experience, we were sent to Fort Knox to perfect our non-existent experiences as clerk typists, a crucial qualification for wartime duties. Hungry, all of us would find time to eat in Lexington Ky, which reminds me of an experience I was going to have in the South many summers later; a friend of mine was teaching a summer course at Columbia. One of the adult students invited him to come down to Miles College in Birmingham, an all-black institution down south. He said: "I've got a friend who'se been teaching Négritude. I think some of your students might be interested." She invited me to come along. We took a plane. She met us at the airport. In the car she sort of smilingly warned us not to be apprehensive if we heard shots in the night. "The police like to visit our campus and play with their weapons. It's got nothing to do with you!"

That night we heard gun shots. "Don't take it personally." She had warned us.

Later, the following night, she invited some of her students and one, who worked at night in the coal mines, asked me if I couldn't send him French magazines. There was nothing in the library. The minute I got back to NY, I did send him a package.

Then off to visit a class. I entered. "Has anybody ever heard of Aimé Césaire?" One of the students, a slightly older one, "What's whitey doin' here?" I don't know how I got the nerve to answer but I did: "Either you hear me out or maybe you'd like to step out of the classroom?"

That night, a conscientious objector from the School of Theology at the U of Chicago took us to a basketball game outside town. We entered the basketball stadium. We were the only three whites in the whole place. Saw the French magazine guy. Not a smile of recognition. The college won the game with the last ball dropped in the basket. Got into the conscientious objector's car. Headed for a burger joint. A while later, on a deserted country road, he says, don't mind, but we're being followed by the police. We got to the burger place before the police. Sat at the counter. The waitress ducked below the counter. When I walked in she must'a thought I was one of those Eastern hippies with my long hair. I ducked below the counter. After a while, and nobody else was in the place, I took a glass ashtray and let it drop on the floor. She popped up. I said: "3 burgers, onion rings and a large order of fries and three cokes." At that very moment two cops came in. She didn't say a word, else we would have spent the night in jail, especially if they had found out the three whities had something to do with Miles College.

When our three day stay was over, we took the plane back to NY. I've got to admit it: it felt like we had been away weeks and weeks, the tensions, the pleasures, the food, the talks, even the teacher who had invited us to her house for drinks and supermarket cheese.

Fort Knox. There I faked playing with the keyboard of an old typewriter. Wrote a couple of love letters written for a couple of soldiers (see above for samples). They told us we were going to Korea. The train ride was long: from Lexington to Chicago then off to Seattle. We did all that train shit.

US Eighth Army HQ in Seoul, not far from the Northern Gate, not far from the dilapidated RR station. I worked in the orderly room, screening anti-syphilis documentaries, but they had been filmed years ago when the lead actor still wore a tricorned hat, looking like Marianne Moore. "Guys, don't shack up with local broads. You'll get a fine case of the clap and then penicillin up your ass and a forced stay in a barracks hospital. Don't do it. It'll also get on your record and when you'll want to get a job, anybody with proper eyesight will see you fucked around in Seoul." The guys laughed. I fast forward and rewound. Put the doccumentary back in its circular steel box.

Every morning my sarge greeted me in the following way: "Hey, Gavronsky, tell us what happened on August 13th, 1893 in Mongolia?" "Sarge I don't know." Then he would break out in a diabolical laugh and say: "See, and he went to collesht!" This lasted for a couple of weeks. Question, no answer, laughter. Then one morning he sends me to unload desks out of a truck. A captain stands by. "OK, put these desks in the Quonset hut in front of you." The captain, perspicacious, looks at me. "Soldier," he says in my direction, "were you ever in Paris?" How the hell could he say that? "Yes, captain, I was." "Well," he says, "that's where I honeymooned. Do you know the Sorbonne Hôtel on rue Victor Cousin?" "Of course," I replied. "Know it well. Stayed there a couple of nights." He was delighted. Told me he had taught European history at West Point, but something had happened: he didn't want to elaborate. And here he was, heading G2 (Current Events). He asked me if I knew how to type, "Of course, captain," and then he said and all this "he said" and "I said" became too much of a routine (except when I needed it) and I swore to myself to cut all that narrative crap out of my novel. Henceforth, no more "he" or "she"... On the spot I was given a desk job inside the Quonset. I later found out the sergeant, from Jamaica, had cut orders to send me to the 38th parallel, where, when it rains, even boots float down rivulets. Saved by my lying about a Parisian hotel!

Lunch time, the captain turned to me and insisted all newspapers on everybody's desk had to be covered. Mamasan had a broom and he could'a sworn she had a camera hidden in it. What was there to provide North Korean intelligence? All we did was check out the South Korean English language newspaper and cut out articles which might have been of a negligible significance to some ignorant bastard in Washington or Langley. When my captain rotated back to the States, and his "turtle" arrived, the first question he asked was: "did their national assembly have vacations like our Congress?" (and that with a heavy southern accent.) The photograph on the curved wall had a picture of some National Assembly people, wearing dark blue suits and ties (the blue suits had been custom-made in Hong King by some poverty-stricken tailor). They almost looked like elected American Congressmen. I was the last to leave the quonset, checking out mamasan and her broom stick, having judiciously covered all our secrets.

For Thanksgiving, we all pitched in and bought her a forty pound turkey, which she could hardly pick up, but immediately went to the local black market and sold it.

Then, with Paul, my army buddy, off for a week-end in Tokyo. But the plane, out of gas, landed in Kyushu and when we got out, we found ourselves on a military base, arrested, since we didn't have the needed papers or Japanese currency. Yet again, the commander, in whose presence we found ourselves, after dutifully saluting, relieved us of all demands placed on ourselves, if we promised to get back to the base no later than 18 hundred hours. We did come back, but in the meantime we hired a Japanese Tourist Guide, the cutest little English-speaking broad. Off we went to a factory which hadn't been destroyed by our accurate bomb-dropping bombadiers. The factory made porcelain toilets and bathtubs. The men wore masks. I've got a great photograph of all of them firing porcelain.

On our second week-end, this time official, we checked into an undistinguished hotel. "Please sign in." The fat lady, with a knowing smile, turned the guest book around: we could read the list of overnight guests: Mr. and Mrs. F. D. Roosevelt, Mr. Churchill and friend, F. Mitterand and his (illegitimate) daughter, Ema Overy. That night we couldn't sleep. On the other side of the rice wall, an old man never stopped talking and she would only repeated: "So deska" or something like that (I wasn't sure of the spelling). Every time she uttered that same formula, she would say it in a different manner, with a different intonation, as she too made a parallel speech. The same-one sided conversation during a cormorant moonless night fishing near Nara: a whole litany of "So deskas," but each response indicated yet another reaction, yet another commentary.

Walking on the sidewalk, I seem to remember, it may have been Kobe, children moved into the street to let us pass. We, of course, ate Kobe beef. You cut it with a fork. Bulls are fed corn, massaged. After that memorable meal, I started smoking again, having given up three prior times.

Upon my return, "my" captain, as I now called him, wishing to go beyond European history, when he returned after lunch, recited the following:

"What is the meaning of a word?"

Let us attack this question by asking, first, what is an explanation of the meaning of a word; what does the explanation of a word look like?

"You'll never guess who I was quoting?"

My answer: "Wittgenstein's Blue Book, the first page."

The captain was astounded. "But you're just a clerk typist!"

Asthma Writer
aesthetic Jewish (m/f)
work   publish
1913 Du côté de chez Swann
1918 A l'ombre des jeunes filles en fleur

I answered in the above series. "Captain, O my Captain, I thought I might give you a hint. Typing is a necessity but so is culture…"

Interviewer: "How many books do you own?"

SG: "A couple of thousands. When I retire, what the hell am I going to do with all that stuff? I don't really know. Maybe I'll get one of those used books guys on Broadway and 111th street?"

Interviewer: "Here's a more personal question. Friends of mine asked me to ask you. Here goes nothing! Have you ever had an affair with any of your students? Touched one of them, dreamt about one of them?"

SG. "A couple of years ago, a friend of mine asked me the same question, adding, wow, an all girls-school! You've got your pick! Got a couch in your office? How about a strong letter of recommendation in exchange?" (Hadn't one on the staff done the same?)

"No" I answered. "You've got to hand it to me! Take those students with mini-skirts uncrossing their legs. Someone once gave a class lecture on the multiple reasons Tristan placed a sword between himself and Iseult."

Interviewer: "Any favorite poets?"

SG. "You've probably not heard of any of them, but here's my list starting with Louis Zukofsky, Francis Ponge, Rilke (maybe you've heard of him?) Guillevic, Marcelin Pleynet.."

Interviewer: "Any contemporary Americans?"

SG. "Michael Palmer, Cole Swenson, Norma Cole…"

Interviewer: "Language Poets?"

SG. "Not at this time. But I greatly appreciate photographers like Hujar…and especially Pierre Molinier and Hans Bellmer. Industrial Gursky doesn't impress me at all."

Interviewer:"Movies?"

SG. "I hardly see U.S. movies anymore. Hung up on naturalism: check out "The Squid and the Whale." If you like post-Zola getting into your bedroom or your living room or on the tennis court, go ahead. Maybe that's why the movie is such a success. Americans rarely have taste in films."

Interviewer: "Last question: Have you ever cried?"

SG. "Sometimes. When somebody tells me they've just returned from a Choate summer in Spain and I've got to flush their pills down the toilet. Then I cry. Sometimes, I don't even know why, I weep. Is it when I hear the Marseillaise? Or when somebody close to me dies? A pretty common reaction, I mean reaching for a Kleenex."

One day, I see "my" captain looking forlorn. "Anything I can do?"

"Let's see what you can do with this letter."

"My sweet Captain,

One night, as I was walking alone down our street, the street where there're only colonels, a black and white poodle siddles up to my ankle. Fearing you know what, I was about to kick it (did you ever see Buñuel's "L' âge d'or?") when a commanding voice called out, 'come here immediately!" That servile beast ran over.

He came towards me. Many excuses; then asked me if, as

his way of excusing himself, I would join him for a drink. I accepted.

Drinks followed drinks. I guess he took me by surprise. He showed me his bedroom. I fell head over heels in a passionate, well I don't usually use vulgar words but this time, in a Rabelasian mood, I did say "fuck." A long time had elapsed since a man's body was on top of me. We removed the bed cover, pushed the sheets aside, placed the pillows in an advantageous position and then followed suit. Naked, in the half-light of a dimming moon, I waited. He didn't take long to penetrate even though, not having had sex for a long time, I was rather dry. He huffed and he puffed until he came. He spurted out on the sheet. I uttered a cry I hadn't heard for a long time and then we rested until he began all over again!"

(I wondered about that. Was it the principle of repetition? I knew that repetition, in the long run, becomes a litany, something preempted of meaning. Was it the same for mimickry? But then again, here I thought that that depended on a previous model. Something had to be "mimicked." In any case, questions arose when he wanted to "begin all over again.")

The poodle pissed on the velvet couch.

Time for us to turn on the light so that we could see each other's bodies.

"Can I light a Havana?"

He went to his desk, opened an elegant wooden box. Took one out. I vocalized in a military fashion: "Stand at ease, soldier! That Havana looks like your penis at attention!" Vulgarity seemed to have taken over!

Fig. I. Shows that before pleasure, gratification is always less than the tension; more than that, it increases the tension. Only the end-pleasure fig. 2 does the energy discharge equal the tension."

"Impossible for you to identify, no?"

"It comes from Wilhelm Reich, The discovery of the Orgon, The function of the Orgasm." (NY: The Noonday Press, 1968 (many previous prints), p. 35 (actually a Division of Farrar Straus & Giroux).

Can you figure out a more exciting quote at the very moment the colonel puffed on his Havana?

Hope you'll find a suitable military personnel to keep you warm during those horribly cold Korean winters.

Sincerely, the one who once upon a time would have added "yours."

He looks at me. "What do you think I should do?"

"How about the three following suggestions? 1. Drive up to the 38th parallel and see the Diamond Mountains. 2. Hitch a ride, disguise yourself as a corporal, and go to the southern most city, not far from where Korean women dive for pearls. And 3. Get hold of a well-dressed Korean prostitute and talk to her for hours about your plight. If you pay her, she'll listen to anything!"

"What an undergraduate solution!"

"I'll answer her letter."

"Dear Lilea, what an expected surprise! I do know my colonel street and can well imagine when the moon dips, desires flair up. I further acknowledge that, in the absence of yours truly, necessity calls, especially that non-Wittgensteinian one! I expect your colonel has seen duty in Vietnam and, before that, when MacArthur crossed the Yalu. Ask him, just to make sure those medals were not purchased on the Tokyo black market! You ask how I'm taking all of this matter in your letter, well, I've had other letters from you (though rare ones!) and if you believe me, I was waiting for this one since…I too have been living off base with a stupendous lieutenant colonel, responsible for all supplies in South Korea. She's been here a year and was in a longing position when I met her in the officers' club. We drank. We danced. We went to my barracks and, to use your single Rabelaisian vulgar word, we fucked like I never did with you! We've been together ever since! That makes almost six months of uninterrupted sex! Can you believe it? She even appreciates my quoting Wittgenstein in bed, at the crack of dawn, no less."

The questions: "'What is length,' 'What is meaning?' 'What is the number one?' Do you see how applicable those questions are to me right now?"

I can also tell you about our trip to Macao and the magnificent banyan trees along the main avenue, not far from the casino. We did a bit of gambling. On an upper balcony, Chinese gamblers threw their moneys in a lowered wicker basket. It landed near the dice game. We didn't win a thing, but the spectable was worth the boat ride from Hong Kong!

Out of common decency, I'll spare you all that you described so accurately in your letter, but just to commemorate my own experience, we did more or less what you did but perhaps with more passion, since she indeed held a higher rank than mine and, as a consequence, in her imaginative needs, invented more than the usual games! I hadn't had such a consistently good time in years, since I seem to recall your activities in bed were...well, let's say, of a minor engagement.

Not 'yours' truly,
Joel."

He also decided to check out the pearl-diving women off that island down south, bringing back to his Lieutenant Colonel a sample, much to her unexpected delight.

This military liaison lasted as long as his "time" in Seoul. They promised each other that, back in Georgetown, they'd manage to continue a spotless arrangement even if her one star general of a husband still demanded once in a while similar treatments. At times he even thought he smelled sperm on her body. She said it was French perfume.

All were happy, as it turns out. Even the poodle got accustomed to Leila.

Did you ever see Buñuel's "Chien andalou?" and I pick that up since we have already alluded to another of his ground-breaking films. Well, apart from Desnos's La Liberté ou l'Amour. That film has meant a great deal to me in thinking about narrativity and the way this novel is constructed with a notable difference, since my title actually allows, as a micro-thematic entrée, a sign of what is to follow whereas, and it may have been Lorca's term, Buñuel never worked out the title of his film. What did I get out of that screening, or those multiple screenings? In the first instance, though I didn't follow his lead here, the discontinuity between title and text. In the second instance, and for me a crucial lesson, the disconcerting play on time zones as well as the unexpected places of action. Thirdly, apart from the restructuring of the narrative, the ideological message: such a humorous critique of the Church (as was his wont in a church-controlled Spain. Buñuel did say that, without Catholicism, he would never have had the energy to do what he did!). Then the wildness of his representation of a reconstructed reality where dream sequences, interruptions, became the norm, everything I had ever suspected had to be in a "novel" which wouldn't look like a novel, but which could captivate a reader, well, some readers!

Besides, Dali had also something to do with that cocktail shaker in lieu of a doorbell or ants crawling in the palm of a hand (did he actually dream that up?) Linda Williams's book, Figures of Desire, did a fantastic job in analyzing Buñuel's films. Or should I say "inspirational"? The proof of the film: there are other ways of seeing screen action besides the commercial shit we see too often in darkened places, some of them used to be palaces in NY. When we'll have another Depression, maybe whole families will go to the movies and see coming attractions, musical shorts, two features and, to boot, a whole orchestra rising from the depth like the Beacon's, one of the last ones to have that sort of a stage. Most of those extremely talented musicians, Russian and Polish Jews, went to Hollywood and played background music for U.S. films. (When I lived at 525 West End Avenue, we had a violinist who played in CATS. He came from Poland, left in 1937. Came here. Then went there (Hollywood). You could hear him practicing late at night not for the show but in order to perfect himself, as if he were still at the Conservatory in Warsaw.)

Back to me or rather to my question: I too have an existence, figuring myself as the "Other" won't do.

"To forget my tiredness, I let my mind go free. Short poems formed in my head to the rhythm of our march and I would run over them, hour by hour, till..." (Claude Lévi-Strauss, Tristes Tropiques, translated by John Russell (NY: Atheneum, 1965, p.337.)

As Thanksgiving neared, I thought I might, and unexpectedly, inform my Korean students at the English Language Institute, where I taught at night after the flag was lowered and we were "free" to take a communal taxi downtown. In my Institute there were twenty students, some of them working for the government. All sat on small wooden chairs; in winter-- and Korean winters are notoriously cold!--we filled an old stove with local wood. Kim Yu Ho knew by experience just how to get that "thing" working without smoking us all out of the classroom. The course book was antiquated by at least one dynasty. As a result, I usually provided students with topics of discussions which pleased me in particular, but as I got to know the twenty and their particular interests, we were, all of us, able to devise intellectually interesting topics such as the place of US troops in Seoul, or the relation between men and women in Korea...

One morning the captain calls a group of us to the orderly room.

The captain: "I've read your dossiers, and if you still believe you're a bunch of nuts, only fit to peal potatoes, then stay the back of the room. On the other hand, after we've had such a pleasant introduction to military life at Fort Dix, some of you may change your mind and rethink your questionable definition. Gavronsky, for instance, is it still true that you do not like girls? Sometimes like and sometimes dislike your parents? That you are highly aggressive? Let me know right now. The same goes for the rest of you. Step up if you wish to change your status."

15 of us stepped forward.

After that, in Korea, where my aggressiveness was fully downgraded, I had an opportunity of being chosen to visit the President of the Republic, Sygman Rhee. Three of us got properly dressed and were driven to the palace, there to wait at least 15 minutes until the aging Rhee, holding onto his Austrian wife's arm, entered . "Please sit," he nodded. "Do you have any questions? Yes, you, what would like to ask of the president of the Korean Republic?"

"Do you believe, your excellency, that the North may again try to invade your country?"

Rhee: "I'm not, he said with a broken smile, your Drew Pearson!"

After that statement, his wife swept him away, turning back to us and saying, with a thick German accent, "the interview is over." But, she did add, "I'll allow a family picture with Sygman."

I've got that photograph in my office.

Rice fields
Clouds mirrored
Huts and pipes
Women bent in the rice fields
La Bruyère says
No, they're not
Animals they're
Peasants.

The bus driver accelerates. Loud Korean music (elevator type). "On your left, rice fields. On your right, rice fields. Any questions?" He learned English as a truck mechanic on a U.S. base.

He explained: "Is it possible to be monolingual (I am, ain't I?) and speak a language that is not (my) own?"

"That remains for you to demonstrated. Yes, indeed."

Jacques Derrida, Monolingualism of the Other OR the prosthesis of Origin, translated by Patrick Mensah (Stanford UP, 1998, p. 5).

Got off the bus, walked around a village where all the villagers were in the fields except an old man, dressed in white, horse-hair top hat, squatting, holding his long pipe and letting time go by. Was he waiting for death?

Then off to Hong Kong on an R&R, flying out of K14, the Quonset-hutted air base outside Seoul. Korean businessmen were totally Johnny Walker Black labeled drunk. In fact, they had to be "escorted" as they wavered down the plane at Kai Tek airport.

SIX MONTHS LATER

"Joel, I've good news and bad news.

The bad is that my colonel has been reassigned to the WHO in Rome. He left two weeks ago. Our last night together was an awful moment, difficult to look back on it.

I drove him to Dulles airport. I followed his erect walk to the plane. He saluted even though he couldn't see me. Maybe we'll never see each other again or perhaps in a couple of months, who knows? And by that time I'll be able to travel with Leonora (as in Leonora Fini...)

That's the good news. Now, I'm in my 3rd month. Morning sickness: lots of vomiting. Appetite predictable. You may know the joke: pickles!

Why am I writing to you? You'll be the new daddy if you accept, and I hope you'll accept.That small package will cheer us, since a while back the doctor did tell you your sperm wouldn't do the trick. Please let me know by e-mail if all of that is OK with you.

P.S.

Rocka bay bee

On the tree top..."

His reply by e-mail.

"I will not quote Wittgengstein but here goes with another quote!

"As it is now constituted, the family of marriage without divorce is absurd, harmful, and prehistoric. Almost always a prison. Often a Bedouin tent covering a lurid mixture of old invalids, women, babies, pigs, asses, camels, hens and filth."

Marinetti, Selected Writings, ed. and with an Introduction by R.W. Flint (NY: Farrar, Straus & Giroux, 1972, p. 76).

I'm certainly not suggesting that, after a rather long intermission, our marriage should mirror the above quote, but I just thought you might enjoy it!

Anyway 'my' Lieutenant Colonel, with a bare bottom, is bound for San Diego, some Army or was it Naval or some retirement home for veterans to be discreetly watched over in case terrorists consider that area fit for a suicide bomber (s).

She is assigned to protect that area with barbed wire, dogs, machine gun towers, roving jeeps with walkie-talkies, as we used to call them!

But I do accept and promise to be a good father despite my inadequate sperm count.

When Leonora is old enough to travel, the three of us will go to Paris and stay at the Sorbonne Hôtel, close to the Luxembourg gardens and especially to the kids' playground, the puppet show and the little outdoor restaurant where the three of us can order ice-cream!

Before I sign off, here's a wonderful story. One day Paul and I decide to eat on the top floor of the Bando Hotel, 'centre ville.' Before we enter, we get our boots shined and Paul looks down into the beautiful eyes of a shoe-shine boy. Love at first sight. Then begins a horrendous search for his father in order to get permission To take him back to the States. His father answers the US military authorities, but they also insisted on finding out his age by checking out his bones. He was, as it turned out, 12 years old, the necessary age for exportation. Yes, he was.

Sometime later, we went to see his place. I'd say 12 tatamis, one for each boy who'd go out to work and then upon their return turn over the money to the old lady who bought cocaine for her supper. Paul was profoundly disgusted. Returned and brought him a US army blanket. She sold it on the black market. Paul took the boy under his wing and got a cot for him in the supply room where he worked, giving out guitars to soldiers who knew how to pay.

Paul wrote to his parents in Neuburg, NY, announcing this boy was on his way and would they come and greet him at Kennedy?

The family got there on time. Kim got off the plane. The family was there. They waved at him as he came through customs. Embraced by his new parents. Then into an impeccable Cadillac, and off to Neuburg where he was given his room.

The parents wrote back.

"Dear son,

Unexpected gift but remember your two other brothers and yourself will have to share the inheritance. Also got to tell you that Kim, every morning, perhaps faithful to his previous work, spit shines the Cadillac as he does all the shoes in my store.

Little did he suspect that he had been adopted by an observant Jewish family. We had him circumsized .Later gave him violin lessons. Kim grew up fast. He went to camp. Fell in love with an elderly lady with three kids whom she sees twice a year in Florida. He told us he wanted to follow her there. We discouraged him.

He became a tennis coach and then he told us he wanted to become a doctor and return to Korea to help his people. I'm ahead of my story, sort of a fast forward story! He did find a Staten Island false blond. We had an officiating rabbi do his thing on our lawn. They settled in Hawaii where Kim became a specialist in farm machinery, going around helping farmers do better with their crops."

I saw him once when he came to my office. Sat on the swivel chair and told me he didn't know what to do with his life. I suggested he take a battery of tests which might specify what were his true talents, even if it meant driving a cross-country truck. He turned to me and returned to his elderly lady with three kids, now growing up and going to school.

In Neuburg, the local paper photographed him and interviewed him especially after his solo violin concert. And that was that.

Paul and I had an R&R coming up. We both decided to see India, Thailand and Cambodia.

We entered the Officers' John: saw a high ranking pilot quietly pissing, perhaps thinking about something else at K 14; Asked him where he was going. Answer: "Bangkok on a SEATO mission." He was willing to take us there. Was he thinking, before zippering up his fly, about college tuition or after-school activities and those unwanted expenses, after all, even as a high ranking pilot, he still had to think about expanding rather large sums of money, especially since his wife didn't work, to take care of her two young ones and two in college. He knew that in the US it was better to be either a millionaire (granted considerable tax breaks from D.C,) or very poor in order to benefit from all those government subsidies. But the middle class!

He also knew his wife to be faithful. And the proof was his long-time service in Vietnam, or "Nam" as his buddies called it. He remembered (all the time "remembering") without telling his friends back home, what it was really like over there; he nearly stopped pissing in his tracks when he saw US troops entering a so-called Vietcong village, massacring the men, old and young, doing the same for all women who didn't want to be raped and, worse of all, bayoneting pregnant women. Who in the hell wanted to foster a future generation of insurgents! If you're a moral human being, wouldn't you have all those American killers face a court-marshal? Hadn't the Japanese in Manchuria done exactly the same, bayonnettes and all? And then, he asked himself, was the Japanese Prime Minister too eager once a year to render homage to the fallen soldiers, the very ones who had been the most violent ones? Then again hadn't Ike visited Bitburg where, alongside "good" German soldiers, SS and Gestapo were buried?

When he was asked, back home on leave, he would only say how many joints he had smoked to get his ass ready for an attack in order to yell: "Kill!Kill!Kill!" as all of them had been trained to scream, charging at straw men with slanted eyes?

"Excuse me sir, is there a possibility to hitch a ride with you to Bangkok?"

"Soldiers, when you address a superior, stand straight and salute."

We saluted.

"As a matter of fact, I do have room for the two of you. You'll have to sit opposite one another. It's a cargo plane bringing very important material to our boys on a SEATO exercize." Though we didn't know it, we had to make a stop-over on a secret US air force base outside Manila to unload our secret cargo: carrots and cases of vodka, the first for vegetarians, the second as a morale booster. Not enough when the officer in charge spotted us. "You guys must be inoculated before going any further." So, arms bare, we walked through a barrage of male nurses needling us in each arm, unloaded god knows what to make sure we didn't catch some terrible disease in those uncivilized places we were going to visit. "Keep moving!" Maybe I was just a weakling, a Columbia College grad. drafted by my own "fucking draft board."

We never got to Manila but we should have. We could smell a whole roasted pig for some family reunion. We would have loved drinking local rhum and even watch Josephine's uncle and his trained cock fighters go at it! Only from the air were we able to check out the action below, what an understatement! Fly over the Philippines, see those forests, those small villages, places where Communist guerillas would one day seriously menace the government. We had forgotten Korea, the Quonset huts, even my Frenchified captain. We did think about getting laid in Manila--too late.

As in a conventional novel, I should now make you hear the hum of engines, those slow movements as we taxied down the field, the jerky take-off. A plane totally stripped of all forms of imagery, kinetic energy, as if the plane had no mind, no sensitivity. A form in space.

We landed on the tarmack in Bangkok. A lurching halt as heavy as Richard Serra's Tilted Arc.

As the burning sun set, the plane evaporated in the dusk, ceding its hard-edged profile to memory. "It could have been a disaster. Related to the plane's forgetfulness, forgetfulness without memory..." (Maurice Blanchot, L'écriture du désastre (Paris: Gallimard, 1980, p. 3.)

There, other planes on the ground, feeding off detritus like hungry condors in the Grand Canyon. But the planes addressed each other as opponents at night, preparing for a rousing, jousting tournament. We were already far away in a rickshaw, wondering if the runner might collapse at night, with only a couple of dollars to his name, and his wife shouting "not enough to buy rice for your five children!" We hardly looked at his legs, rather at the countryside and then the streets, then the crowded klongs with fruits and vegetables sold from large flat boats--the women screaming out their goods, their children packaging them. The next morning, out of our hotel, we hired the same rickshaw and went visiting the gold Buddha and all other tourist sites. I did think about the coming fight on the airfield when not a single human being would witness those horrendous crashes as wings hit wings, propellers, fuselages, and then the whole side of a plane collapsing and not a single human being there to witness the massacre! Were there any female figures in this struggle? What about the delicacy of a single engine plane, or a fastidious interior? For some, it might have looked like a soirée or worse still, an eighteenth-century salon with Mme so and so and at times a heavier customer, let's say, Turgot flamboyantly shocking those highly intelligent women who, masochistically, enjoyed a critique of wealth. Theirs.

With the oncoming of the morning haze, we were back on the tarmack.

From Bangkok we flew to Cambodia on a single engine plane; the pilot's mouth was a jewelry store with lots of gold teeth. At Phnom Pen airport, we were the only plane there. Found a hotel. Our bed had a mosquito netting. A bottle of water cost $35.00 and don't even ask the price of French champagne!

The following morning, we got a rickshaw to peddle us to Angkor Wat, a place Malraux would have so wished to rob and take back to his Paris abode! The ears of the Buddha were enormous: he could hear everything tourists were saying but apart from three Germans and ourselves, there wasn't a single soul out there. Outside, patiently waiting, centuries of waiting, dressed in safran robes, four religious guys with their copper begging bowl in hand, hoped for some contribution. Otherwise, on a strict rice diet. Well, somebody on a diet might have been quite content. If it hadn't been for French archeologists, chopping away at a huge forest, we wouldn't ever had seen those larger palaces making Versailles look like a pygmy hut.

Back in Bangkok, we checked into the same hotel which had a Swiss chef. I didn't get sick to my stomach but Paul, who always claimed he had an iron cast stomach, got so sick we had to call the hotel's doctor for shots.

From there, off to Calcutta where we couldn't land. A plague or something, so we got back on the plane and flew to Delhi. All I could say immediately was "long live colonialism!" Broad avenues, clean hotels, cheerful people, decent food, handsome women in their saris. We visited old Dehli and the Red Mosque. A guide stood before a group of us. "See this little box? It has a red hair from Buddha's head. If you want to take picture, five dolla." He smiled. I pulled out a single red hair from my head and gave it to him. "Let's compete!" I muttered. He didn't have my NY sense of humor. I truly believed for a moment he would yell for the police to intervene as if I had personally insulted Buddha's hair. He didn't.

We left rather quickly and off we went, with an official guide, trained by local authorities and wearing a badge to prove it. From Korea we had hired a limousine which we found waiting at the front door of our hotel, and the guide inside together with a handsomely dressed chauffeur. Drinks in the trunk, endless talk in the front. "Do you see those numbers on tree trunks?" Of course we did. "That was inscribed by the Brits when they were here." He smiled. (Good riddance to the Brits, his smile seemed to say). At a later moment, we came across a number of local citizens, fixing huge nets and begging for money. Kids swarmed all over the windshield. We took our required pictures and told the driver to ignore all of them and speed ahead. Our next stop was Phati Sikripour, that magnificent and deserted palace with a second floor meant to allow the big chief to avoid the morning heat, surrounded by his lovely girls. Unfortunately for him (them?) the place ran out of water and, as of that instant, they all had no other recourse but to hie back to Old Delhi where the maharajah had a splendid town palace, constant servants and a large enclosed swimming pool, surrounded by exotic trees and plants. Always a ready servant to serve guests with forbidden European drinks and exotic fruits.

How long did we stay in Delhi? I've forgotten, but our next stop was the Taj Mahal at a precious moment when the moon was full and, consequently, the palace lit up and the marble talked in various hues. We made ourselves as comfortable as possible on the grounds. At one moment the father of a handsome Indian family turned to us and asked for the time. "Why did he address us in English?" Our guide answered: "There are over 200 languages in India and he may only know 20, so English is still the 'lingua

Britannica'."

The return trip was uneventful. We already had been to Tokyo, seen the Kegon Falls, wandered around Kyushu. We had eaten in the finest restaurants in Kyoto and observed bent-over old ladies picking stray flowering weeds. What more was there to do for us on our second R&R?

SIX MONTHS LATER

A rare case of the clap. (was it ever rare?). Penicillin. Dossier has it all. Was it that prostitute on the DMZ who only asked to have me read her lover's letters, an American sergeant who promised to re-enlist for a fourth tour of duty in Korea? Could it have been one of the ones in town, or perhaps even one of my beautiful older students, a handsome low-class government official? I never went further in my guessing game. All I knew was I had found myself once again in Fort Dix turning in my gear. Nobody questioned anything, just letting me know that, instead of serving the required 18 months, it really wasn't worth the government's time to ship me out to Missouri, for example, since a couple of months later, in any case, I would be discharged.

What had we learned during all those travels? Well, that practically nobody whom I knew had visited these places and that nobody came home with such an immense number of color slides to be shown when I removed Koschmider's large painting over the dinner table and made in its place the equivalent of a screen. Then the sliding of the tray so that, manually, I could go through a great number of slides, especially those taken in Korean rice fields, huts, people, foods and the bullet pock marks on nearly every downtown buildings where most of the fighting had occurred. I compared them with the government buildings on St. Germain, on the way to the Seine. One day I would screen all those slides for my grand-children even though, as Proust had noted, in an album there is no continuity. We would go from slide to slide and in between a blank.

André Breton writes that he had to learn: "une faible partie de ce que j'ai oublié. » (André Breton, Nadja (Paris : Folio/ Gallimard, 1964, p.10.) That's the way memory works.

If I collected all those images, encounters, pleasant memories, acting like so many sub-titles, I had others I could just as easily show you, and you might say, in reality, all those souvenirs were like a recurring dream of little importance.

By comparison, there are innumerable travels at the heart of writing itself, or at the very least, on a metaphorical level. If you like to read, there's always Homer for the West and Monkey for India, or in France, Diderot's Supplément to Bougainville's Voyage or again John Steinbeck's Travels with Charlie. By comparison, my story seemed rather bland, much like a bucket lowered down a well with hardly any water left at the bottom. By comparison, my great grand-father's travels were far superior to my own peripatetic ones.

In my life, I never actually suffered.

Unlike those American movies showing Parisians escaping the Nazi onslaught, finding themselves on a country road: cars, trucks, at times horse-drawn carriages, and lots and lots of families walking, trying to escape straffing German planes. Those pilots had most likely been trained during the Spanish Civil War. What did I leave behind? We left Paris, heading for Clérac, where my French-born aunt's father, a smith, worked and harvested his grapes in September. Then off to Bordeaux, Marseilles, and then Lisbon, with a stop-over to see the Prado in Madrid. I can still remember what I thought was an endless Atlantic crossing. My father said it had taken 18 days to get to NY, since our Portuguese boat, which should have carried 300 passengers, took in as much money as a 1000 passengers could pay. My father slept on a wooden plank placed over a bathtub. Why in fact do I remember all the above? Probably nothing that I could acknowledge because of a deep memory: my father had told me all about it.

Well, I did leave my sail boat in one of the basins in the Luxembourg Gardens (the Tuileries only had one, but a big one!) I left behind all my toys, my books (my paternal grandmother had given me the complete Jules Verne), my room, the early morning perfume of bread being baked, and early Sunday mornings, when the baker prepared "visit" pies for the family. I left the "charcutrie" with those beautiful stuffed tomatoes ready to poison me when the sun came out and curdled the mayonnaise. Left behind the clicking noise of the maid's high heel shoes who, every morning, crossed the courtyard and hid herself in the kitchen to change into her apron and other shoes. One day, I was so curious, I smashed down the opaque window, but she had already gotten dressed!

Years later, my mother, glancing at the "French Review," spotted the name of one of my childhood friends: he too had had a sailboat. We met. We compared war stories. He had gone to Cuba and then to NY, now he was a retired professor of French and Spanish at Princeton. He had three boys. I had one daughter. He had married a German girl. He wanted to know what I had done in the meantime. Those are either the silliest questions or the most innocuous ones. I married an Austrian girl whom I had met in the Luxembourg Gardens, sitting on one of those stone benches between two elderly equestrian masters who attacked each other's techniques. The police blew their whistle. The park was to close. I went out with Anne-Marie and that was the beginning, the first step which landed us in my maid's room at 107 blvd. Raspail. I better stop here!

My grandfather had been very active on the Socialist side before and during the first Russian Revolution. Under that short-lived Kerensky regime, he had been named mayor of Moscow, and then he accepted the leadership of the Duma, their version of parliament.

Had I done anything slightly ressembling such a life-long political-humanist career? Nothing of a similar weight. I did read my anti-war poems against the war in Viet-Nam. I read my poems together with my friends on the Lower East side. The Judson Church, St. Marks-in-the Bowery, and once on a platform driven by a truck in Central Park. I read with Jackson McLow, one of the most fantastic poets I have ever known. I went to Washington, I signed petitions, I screamed anti-war slogans, I must have waved in unison huge anti-war posters. I even must have been photographed at one of those Living Theater productions when the theater was located on 14th street, before they were thrown out of the US for not paying their taxes. I guess I could now check my files under the Freedom of Information Act. But, like my friend's dossier, most of the juicy parts would have been blackened out, much like those post-cards written by prisoners of war: I ....you Think...Hugs...Here...

Could this be too much of a self-denigrating portrait? Yes, if you compare me with what my grandfather had lived through. Below I've taken out a couple of pages from his Memoirs of a Soldier of the Russian Revolution (1883-1895), published in Paris in 1933. (Perhaps even that title encouraged me...) before you read this, let me remind you that he came from a solid middle class Jewish family, that he had been one of the only Jews allowed to study at the Gymnasium (much like my father), that he had enrolled at the university and there, at one of those rare political meetings, he had been spotted by agents of the tzar's police who arrested him shortly thereafter. Now to my grandfather's memoirs.

"......After a time, we were taken on foot to the prison where we were to stay for eight to ten days until the orders for our final destination arrived. For some it was western Siberia; for others, eastern Siberia. We stopped at the prison gates and our "starost," who suspected we might be split into smaller groups, insisted we be shown our cell.

.....

The situation, to say the least, was embarrassing: there was neither water nor latrines and, what's more, men and women were together in the same cell...

.....

We made preparations for the next leg of the journey—the march from Tomsk to Irkutsk.

There were no railroads out there. We were going to travel on foot a distance of 2500 versts (about 1650 miles total—Ed.)But we were young. Nothing scared us. We started out at the end of June. There were about 40 of us—criminals with families, and ourselves—all going to eastern Siberia.

.....

Our guards treated us with the greatest severity. ...The soldiers warned us that, at the slightest attempt to escape, they would fire upon the whole group.

.....

The trip was exhausting. Day after day we had to walk in dust, heat, and clouds of insects which bit us incessantly....They slipped into our ears, noses, eyes, mouths...

.....

A whistle blew. Out of bed. Back on the road.

"How far are we from Irkutsk? We've had enough. Let's get to that rotten hole we're going to have to live in."

And once again we were back on the road to the unknown.

.....

Exhausted as we were by this journey that had lasted seven months, it was difficult to satisfy our comrades's curiosity about the situation in Russia. Besides, we had brought mostly sad news. The movement, the "Will of the People," crushed by the police in 1881-1883, was now trying to revive itself in the south and in St. Petersburg, Riga, and Moscow where they were reorganizing, but without much success, the remnants of dispersed groups. Later on, in 1887, a group of the "Will of the People" emerged for a while but then disappeared. The Social Democrats had laid the foundation for a fledging organization.

(Translated from Russian into French by my mother and I did it from French into English.)

If you're interested in a more succinct portrait, let me quote the biography of my great grand-father, and my grand-father from the Jewish Encyclopedia, p.39. At the top of the page, in caps: MINNESOTA.

MINOR, SOLOMON ZALMAN (Zalkind; 1826-1900)

" Writer and scholar, one of the pioneers of the Russian-Jewish intelligentsia. As a youth, he entered the newly opened government rabbinical seminary in Vilna and was one of its first graduates— he was later a Talmud teacher in his seminary. Through the efforts of the "maskilim," he was elected "kazyonny ravvin" (government appointed rabbi of the Minsk community in 1859). One of the first to preach in Russian in the synagogue, he became well-known for his sermons which were published in book form and served as models for other rabbis. Minor was active in the promotion of "Haskalah" in Minsk, and in 1869, he was invited to serve as rabbi in Moscow. In the early 1890's, when the Jews of Moscow were persecuted, he interceded with the authorities on behalf of his community and was consequently expelled from Moscow on the order of the governor of the city, the Grand Duke Sergei. He then returned to Vilna and continued his literary activity there. Minor published many articles in the Russian-Jewish and Hebrew press, for the most part under the name of "Remez." He conducted a debate with anti-Semites (including the priest Luyostansky) and was a friend of Tolstoy's and, for a short time, directed his studies in Hebrew and the Bible. His son, Lazar (Eliezer) Minor was a professor of nervous diseases, and another son, Ossip Minor, was a leader of the Social-Revolutionary Party."

Now, who can rival with that sort of biography? One day my uncle, the doctor, was asked by one of his white Russian clients, then staying at the Sherry Netherlands Hotel, if he was Jewish. Answer: "No, I'm not, but my grandfather was a rabbi!" Stunned, the very white Russian still needed my uncle to give him a shot in the arm.

Now onto Ossip Minor S. (Joseph: 1861-1932) (he saw me in my crib with a lock of red hair. He looked down and said to my mother, his daughter, "whatever he does, let him learn a manual trade.") He himself was a typographer as so many Russians had been and, in fact, the Russian language newspaper in New York depended on them to get every issue out. If I remember anything about "Novo Ruska Slovo" (Christ, is that the right spelling?), for me, it was that back page where you could read a daily strip of Tarzan comics, the only piece in English.

I took Ossip seriously. When I went to College, I worked in the sub-basement of the Cultural Services of the French Embassy, 972 Fifth Avenue. I worked with a Cuban lady who sent her only son to Cuba. Why? "Because the school in my neighborhood is overcrowded with Puerto Ricans." She taught me to air out reams of paper before slipping them into a multilith machine, something you'd have to purchase in an antique shop today. I made enough to pay for travel expenses.

"Russian revolutionary and a leader of the Social Revolutionary Party. Born in Minsk, he was the son of Rabbi S.Z. Minor (check out the info above). While still a student at the University of Moscow, he joined the "People's Will" (Narodnaya Volya). In 1883 he was arrested for the first time, and in 1887 he was exiled to Siberia. After participating in a rebellion of exiles in Yakutsk he was sentenced to force labor for life (1889). Freed in 1896, he was banned from European Russia. In 1900 he nevertheless returned to Russia and settled in Vilna. He resumed his revolutionary activities, traveled abroad, and was one of the organizers of the Social Revolutionary Party. In 1909 he was again arrested as a result of the intervention of a czarist double agent, Y.F. Azeff, and was sentenced to ten year's forced labor. He was freed at the time of the 1917 Revolution. Minor left Russia in 1919 after the Bolshevik victory and settled in Paris, where he became chairman of the Society for Assistance to Exiles and Political Prisoners in

Russia. He died in Paris. His book Eto byolo davno ("It was Long Ago") appeared posthumously in 1933.

I've been quoting from the same work redubbed, "Memoirs..."

PARENTHESIS

Walked up Broadway. A transit strike. Millions to pay and shoes to repair. Why? Faces all along Broadway. Ears covered. Smiles effaced: arbitration-- whispers through the cold air. Streets blocked. Would it be the same in case of an "attack"? CIA and FBI listening in. Working. Checking out.

"La Geste du silence»: I've almost finished my poem. Lookin' good. Where shall it go? Paris, no doubt or...Marseilles. (Crumbs from my buttered roll; e-mails from desperation. Helicopters hovering in the sky. Radio messages: highways nearly empty.) Cops in yellow jackets direct traffic. Stop cars on 96th Street when they do not have 4 passengers. Fake ones abound. Stores raided for mannequins for tomorrow's move from the suburbs. Courneuve: "voitures" burning. Lots of them. Helpless government. "Ship them back to where they come from!" Airplanes. Handcuffs. Small packages with "baguettes/saucisson" + butter from Normandy. Cows and graves. Housing projects destroyed or about to be. The Minister of Justice from Hungary should be pronounced "Sharkozy." Booes; applause.

Whoever they are, they're complaining: too many clandestine workers. Put electrified fences all around the country just like they're planning to do between Mexico and the US.

In a barricaded town house. Messages. On the corner, whispering into a T-Mobile: "Don't move! We'll get you out!" Limo at the ready around the corner. Secondary residence. Servants cleaning the master's bedroom. "change the sheets, you fuckers!"

Kitchen. Eggs/ Fries. He likes that for his "petit déjeuner."

People still walking in small groups on Broadway. Who will get to Wall Street before tomorrow? Money is slipping through the coffers of the transit people, now down under as if they were all thinking of Australia. Why not?

Some have remained locked up in Nassau county.

MacArthur airport.

Horses at the ready. Bicycles for rent.

On the side of the highway, going to the Hamptons, buses, franks and burgers on the side of the road.

Who will die? Who will survive?

You can hear the screech of ambulances not moving. Surgeons's tools in hand.

Lunch. Sable, sturgeon, smoked fish and for those with cheaper taste, creamed herring.

More people walking down Broadway. Some whistle. TV crew on 96th st. "Well, what's you prediction?"

A group stationed in front of innumerable banks gather to sing: " We shall Overcome," as if this were a remembrance of a black leader from Chicago.

Food stores raided. In the aisles, women push carriages. Kids scream. Cashiers out-numbered. "Go home! There's nothing left on the shelves."

In the meantime, huskies have been talked into returning into the foray. Sleds can accommodate four passengers. Cost: $50.00 for a short ride: Let's say from 111th st. to 86st. Further downtown: every extra block: $20.00. To Kennedy: $150.00. Cash only.

Music provided to calm nerves at no extra cost.

Is it true Walter Benjamin, before he committed suicide, thought of teaching at Yale alongside Paul de Man, at least before Derrida stepped in?

END OF PARENTHESIS

Addition, working in the first person singular.

I could not have survived had it not been for a handful of jelly beans. I'm quite a discriminating eater, leaving aside (if possible!) the yellows and the orange ones, concentrating on the black ones. I'd say the same for Chuckles. This is not an intense pleasure but on cold days it's sufficient. Perhaps it might recall an involuntary memory and remind me of my grandmother in Marseilles who was always angry when my sister and I showed up around 3:30, telling her we had had a rich lunch near the harbor and, consequently, would not be hungry enough to eat three "tartes aux pommes."

An assortment of other sugary things. Furious. "Why do you do that?"

She slumped in her armchair.

Looked truly distraught. In the meantime, an Italian newspaper was delivered. She had already read both "Le Monde" and the "Manchester Guardian," just to keep in touch with the outside world.

We looked at a recent James Bond. Baku. A wealthy bedroom in a 4 star hotel, a bedroom decorated with a gold-leafed ceiling. "Obscene," D. H. Lawrence once said means "Off Stage." He also claimed that Pascal's Pensées in English came out as "Pansies."

I once ate a cheap burger on the corner of M. Le Prince and St. Michel. Heard students talking about their English seminar. Siddled up to them. "Do you think I might join you? Of course, I'll introduce myself to your professor." "No need," they replied. We entered a large classroom. We sat. An elderly professor walked in. Took off her glasses. Seemed to adjust binoculars in their stead. Opened Tristram Shandy. "Please note: in the first edition on page 38 there is a period. In the second edition, it was replaced by a semi-colon. Very significant."

Students began dozing off. Others made little paper airplanes and shot them over the heads of their fellow students. Soon a considerable snoring filled the air. "In the third edition, note the return of the period which actually was to be replaced by a semi-colon in the fourth edition. Take note. This is very significant." By that time, nobody listened to this "maître conférencière."

When we all trouped out (some had to be awakened from a deep sleep), I couldn't help myself. "Do you realize," I said to them, back at that burger place, "that the passage she chose was a fabulous one?" Nobody cared. "We must spew that period/semicolon on our final exam. That's it. No choice. No deconstruction reading at all!"

Another writer wrote the following: "What prodigious armies you had in Flanders!" which, by the way, reminded me of a wartime British poet included in numerous anthologies of little known poets. "In Flanders Field," and thereafter launched into an orgasmic analysis of: "Was every day in my life to be as busy a day as this..., All that, and in the meantime, "never once lifting (this) eye from the ground where one man moves as one man." Fracturing this fluidity, this melifluous passage, he knew when to shoot, where to hide, when to run through deserted streets of a small village in the North of France. Or, as in a film, rush through narrow Berlin streets where he would have to wait for his contact and, in that black car, make his way to the bridge and reach "Check Point Charlie."

He waited. Lit an East German cigarette. Coughed in his hat. Thought of alliterations. Quoted a poem by Edward Taylor:

But a mighty, Gracious Lord,
Communicate
Thy Grace breaks the cord afford
Thy Glorys Gate
And the State.

On a more somber note, not far from Auschwitz, recalled Sigfried Sassoon, who quoted a war correspondent: "The effect of our bombardment was terrific. One man told me he had never seen so many dead before."

In the meantime, Bond charged through a huge oil pipeline just about to blow up with a nuclear warhead inside. "Sang froid."

Marvelous dexterity. A female companion. A scientist disarmed the bomb. Ran to the Blue Mosque where they found a huge cache of Beluga caviar. (Now almost beyond anyone's wallet even at Zabar's) The plot goes on and on and on.

I do remember, in another flick, an old lady whose shoe concealed the equivalent of a knife. She threatened Bond (I've forgotten who played him) who, of course, escaped. What are your memories? I mean your own, private, non-communicated memories?

Switch figures (not of speech!).

Midnight.

Across the street a flashing sign: "Come in! See our girls, enjoy our private booths!"

All of a sudden, I remembered my professor, Lionel Trilling. When he was hired, it is said (true or false?) that the then President of Columbia University spoke clearly to the chair of the English department: "Now that you've got your Jew, don't hire another one." He closed the door behind him. You could hear his every step as he walked down the English department's corridor.

He wrote a beautiful preface to Babel's "Red Cavalry." (Nathalie Babel had just died in the "Times," having served her father over the years, writing, proof-reading, checking out translations. Suffering his absence.)

Trilling was always impeccably dressed, with spit-polished shoes, at least as we expected a college professor to be; teaching in Hamilton Hall, in a room not far from that narrow elevator. "Class and Self," or some course title like that, and off we went with Jane Austen (Emma), Charles Dickens (Hard Times) and D. H. Lawrence (Lady Chatterly's Lover (did you ever see the film?) What do I remember (here we go again!) He had a way of holding his "High Life" cigarette, twirling his glasses. We paid acute attention. (Later on, we learned that Diana Trilling had seen "Deep Throat" with a host of other educated women. Was Susan Sontag one of them? Having digested to the lee Roland

Barthes, her analysis may have been of a more semiotic nature. But who knows?) Later, on a couple of occasions, I met Trilling on Broadway near the now defunct Chock full O' Nuts on the corner of 116th st where I often asked for a raisin bread with cream cheese sandwich. His recognition always touched me as was the case, many years later, with Edward Said, who, by the way, when I once addressed him as "Ed" flew into a minor rage. So proud of his English name (he hadn't always felt that way, by the way…) Years before, he had met my wife and I together with Cynthia at the Tip Toe Inn between 86th and 87th st on Broadway. We sat in the back. A few weeks ago, I sat next to his wife who spoke eloquently about the "situation" in Iran (or was it Irak?) When you get to be my age, there're holes in the memory! but standing on that windy corner on Broadway and 116th st. not only did I meet Lionel Trilling, but much later, in fact, a fantastically wise and gifted scholar, Yosef Yerushalmi, whose wife played Chopin in her living room, and also made a documentary on Chopin, the idol of a certain Parisian crowd. (We all had learned about his brief Venice stay with George Sand (without an "s" in order to appear even more of a masculine figure.) Like Balzac's Sarrasine. (See Barthes's majisterial analysis of that same work).

He was not alone playing with literary figures. André Breton in Marseilles, before landing in Port-au-Prince and, by chance, coming across in a bookstore, Aimé Césaire's "Tropiques" or was it an early edition of Cahier d'un retour au pays natal? When he landed in NY (reminiscent of Ferdinand Céline's own experience), he found friends and a while later was hired to give talks on the "Voice of America" on 57th st. across (or nearly so) the Art's Student's League. My mother worked next to him. When Roosevelt decided to back Admiral Giraud rather than de Gaulle, with principles, my mother quit. She then met an illustrious newly-appointed Cultural Counselor of the French Embassy and was rapidly hired. My mother stayed there for nearly 30 yrs. His name was Seyrig. I played with his daughter who, later on, became one of France's most talented film and stage actresses, Delphine. They lived off Central Park West in a modest apartment. So did we on 107th street off Central Park West, but I think I've already told you that story!

Those who survived Ellis Island were all type-cast by officials:

X for crazy
C for tuberculosis
TC for trachoma
K for hernia

Some came through (after having fingers rammed up their scrotums) to become illustrious professors, writers, poets, and literary critics.

Letters of rejections. Interviews. Rejections.

Some were hired at the New School for Social Research where once Diego Rivera's huge panel was taken down. Too leftist.

Freud lurked in the binding. Darkness of the unconscious revealed. "Partisan Review." Trilling was there. I do not remember the color or the make of his shoes.

Tolstoy was a favorite topic for conversation, often leading to some New Criticism analyses. In his work, The Kingdom is Within You (written between 1890 and 1892), Tolstoy once again defended his ideas of non-resistance to evil by force. He condemned all governments for their oppression of the masses. His other ideas—on private property, against revolutionary movements and on the necessity of striving to accomplish Christian ideals—were all expounded in that work and forcefully so. What about his novel Resurrection, the proceeds of which were to go to the Dukhobors? They say his wife was dissatisfied because that money would not be forthcoming to help his children and grandchildren whom she described as "poverty stricken." By then, Tolstoy was even more estranged from his wife then he had ever been.

And even though (I'm still with Tolstoy) he was not in good health, he continued his drama, "And the Light Shineth in Darkness" (an autobiographical play he never finished).

The war had yet to end. Regular bombs kept on falling. Not one however on the railroads tracks leading to that infamous concentration camp which, in perfect German, proudly announced on top of the main entrance: " Arbeit Macht Frei." Pétain had substituted the Trinity of the French Revolution with his own version of the Vichy government: L'Etat français "Travail, Famille, Patrie." He put up posters of Jews with huge crooked noses; sent French workers to Germany; kissed babies, visited youth labor camps. He also chased young maids in his Vichy hotel. Charles Maurras provided ideology for him. Darlan took care of the French fleet. All were convinced that the "Révolution nationale" would replace, in French commemorative rituals, the first of an endless series of French Revolutions.

Who now teaches that epoch?

The old man, before he died, recovered (perhaps) some of his earlier reputation made at Verdun where, one of his subalterns, was De Gaulle.

On the frontispiece of the local public school in St. Rémy, you could still make out that Vichy trinity.

Dunhill: once again worn on a week day as if the occasion were to be fabricated and so, into the closet where he kept his suits on a wooden hangar and slacks on rods. He slipped the slacks off the rod and removed the vest from a hangar. He looked at himself in the floor to ceiling mirror; straightened out his tie, an inconspicuous one which he had equally removed from the tie rack on the same closet door. Perhaps a darker shade of a regimental somebody had given him on some birthday. He called Diana to help him out. Color blind, he needed someone's opinion before leaving the house. He had picked out, from another closet, a recently purchased white shirt with an Italian collar, a bit more dandyesque, if anyone asked.

He picked up his leather French "cartable," opened and then closed the front door and quickly walked across Broadway to Hamilton hall.

The diminutive elevator lady, who had been there a long time actually remembered, twice a week, what floor he needed. She pushed the fourth button from the top. He could have done the same, but she was a union person and there wasn't the slightest chance of her being either fired or asked to be reassigned. (In any case, with the TWU on strike, this may not have been the ideal moment for either possibilities.)

Once in class, he opened up his "cartable," took out that day's reading and looked over the crowded classroom, checking out who might have skipped class, for he was sensitive to absences, assuming that missing one of his lectures amounted to a form of discrimination, perhaps even an anti-Semitic sign. All were there.

He took out a cigarette, lit it, held it. Placed it in his mouth and, mechanically, as was his wont, started playing with his glasses, quite a trick when you consider that, in the other hand, he held onto his half-smoked cigarette.

"Let us analyze the paragraph on p. 205 of your Harper Classic, Harper & Row Publishers. I would like some feed-back on your reading. (This was not his usual habit).

A bright student sitting in the back of the room raised his hand, but before reading, he said: "let me quote a short passage from Emma. I know you like that novel!"

"But you must have found it very damp and dirty. I wish you may not catch cold.

"Dirty, sir! Look at my shoes. Not a speck on them." (The Complete Novels of Jane Austen (NY: The Modern Library, nd, p.766).

The student repeated the text: "I curse the hour in which I was born to such a destiny."

Trilling smiled. "Please, go on."

"Well, let me begin at the beginning: that is, the apparent allusion to some ancient set-up, I mean the "Curse…" Was it a reminder of a Shakespearian text, what we now might call an intertextual reference, or an appropriation in need of further reflection? I would go the latter road. "Curse," as far as I'm concerned, immediately provides the reader with a radical incipit. I might suggest: "A curse on both your houses" or something like that. I might add that this incipit leads the way to the next syntagma, that is, the non-precision of the hour, or perhaps, had we been previously informed, yet another but this time intratextual reference. "The hour": in this particular instance, it might not only deliberately have been a way of disturbing the classical reading technique, that is, left to right, but with the "hour" unspecified, stop our mechanical mode of traveling, first horizontally and then, proceed vertically, trying to remember what had preceeded our ambulating mode. Was it the "hour" of his doom? A forewarning of a catastrophic and highly limited future or simply a way of hyperbolization, misleading the reader until he or she might become aware of this subtifuge? The next term, "born," provides us, as readers, now well-adapted to the conniving manner of Dickens's writing, with another imprecise, pseudo date, the moment of experiencing birth, as if consciousness were readily available at that exit moment! But in lieu of being "born" from the womb, there is a metonymic switch to "destiny," thereby, once again, and in a mysterious and unscheduled strategy, place in front of "born" a "destiny," or if you wish, to put it in another way, playing with "curse," another referential allusion forcefully leading us back to the original blocking since a "curse" lasts an indeterminate moment of time."

"Good. Any other suggestions?" His cigarette had gone out. He continued playing with his rimless glasses.

"Yes, professor Trilling. I believe I may have another way of analyzing this same text. but knowing your pleasure, let me quote another passage from Emma: "Emma watched her through the fluctuations of her speech, and saw no alarming symptoms of love." (Ibid., p. 779).

"Please, go on."

"I believe the previous reader, by using already antiquated terminology, has radically evinced the heart and soul of the passage which, to my way of thinking, raises a frightening thought, made amply clear in that, since the paragraph is indented and followed by another, right beneath it and, let me quote so that the argument may, perhaps, gain strength. Here is the passage, or at least the beginning of it…"He looked at her in doubt and dread, vacantly repeating 'Curse the hour? Curse the hour?'"

Then he went on with his own review of the first speaker who could have, in his own language, also suggested about "Curse" that there is an anatomical suspicion haunting that so-called "curse" which has been devalued and made into a "human" commentary and therefore justifying "doubt and dread," as well as the totally unexpected "vacantly repeating." This last appreciation of the speaker's troubled reaction leads me to suspect that the above paragraph, in its brevity, hankered to be followed by the "Father," having addressed his daughter, "Louisa." I said a "human touch," and of course, the exaggerated paragraph that my fellow classmate defined does not take into consideration what every good reader already knows and that is the non-independent nature of analyzing isolated words. I've come to that simple conclusion in my translation seminar where, every time somebody comes up with a single word and hopes to have it defined in English, the instructor stops him or her and clearly states that no word ever stands by itself can be properly translated since context is all that counts; I've had that told to me over and over again so that now, when someone accosts me on Broadway and asks me to help her define a single word out of Deleuze's work on cinema, I refuse and request the full sentence. Then and only then can I be of help.

"Fine explanation, but it seems to me that you've misjudged New Criticism. Let that be: I always welcome an unintended analysis."

The bell rang. All of us got up except for the first analyst who ambled over to Trilling's desk in the hope that his presentation might figure, at some later date, in a "Partisan Review" footnote.

Memory's mind.

A lapsus.

He had conveniently forgotten that, as an aspiring instructor, he would have proceeded in that same manner, but it was a bit too late to bring that up.

Trilling left the classroom. He bumped into an old colleague and with him, avoiding the diminutive elevator lady, both decided to walk down from the 4th floor.

"Lionel," he said, "something amusing happened to me yesterday morning as I was glancing at a NY "Times"obit. I not only recognized SG's name but also and much more than that, the name of the one who had written it! That's what I wanted to tell you!"

A pause.

"Fred, now I've forgotten his last name, such things do happen at our age! Anyway, I knew him when he first started at the "Times" writing Obits and that before he transferred to the City Desk (or was it vice versa? I tell you, my memory's abilities are being screened!) Years, ago, he told me how he had been assigned by his boss to investigate SG's life, just to fill in the biographical gaps that would certainly have been caught by his friends.

Now Trilling.

"I too knew him but only fleetingly. As I remember him, he was a jolly good fellow and quite intelligent! My own impressions match yours and Fred confirmed them since he had already gathered a significant amount of information to help him along. Fred...dear Fred (I too have forgotten his last name except it all came back when I read the obit) acted like a private eye. So far the only clue missing was that he didn't look like the young Belmondo, and near him a brash blond in a cheap hotel, manhandled by a thug wearing a Borsolino. Or was she one of those who, finding a tripod, placed her digital on top and chocked herself in an autoerotic gesture?"

Trilling stopped and then went on. "Fred spoke resolutely about his—he called it—monomaniacal undertaking which had begun as an ordinary assignment, a run-of-the mill investigation, and now turned out to be ever-demanding. He spelled out the Roman experience as if he had himself digitally photographed it in order to go further and further toward his yet undefined goal. What eventually seemed to be as crystal clear as a glass made in Morano was…" Here he stopped and evoked James Bond and a lovely scientist lady investigating a batch of highly poisonous "flacons," as he called them. They saw an airplane taking off with the same insignias on the wing. Where was this monster going? How could he be stopped? What weapons were they going to use? Both then crossed one of those curvy bridges in Venice while below a singing gondola ("To Russia with Love," that infamous Spector agent and a lady with a sharp blade coming out of her left shoe), one of those tourist gondolas. A song arose at that very moment. Here Fred stopped.

There were still holes in his portrait of SG's past life. Was what he had gathered simply misinformation, just to throw him off the track? Any odd switching of the first person singular amounted to a conundrum. Fred, with all his graduate studies in the post-modern novel, could never, on his own, fathom such "mélanges" of identities, all meant to throw him off the track or at least make him think twice about the virtues of literature. That convinced him he still had lots of work to do.

One late afternoon, when the sun gilded the horizon, he happened to be strolling in the vicinity of the Villa Medicis where the French government, having selected the youngest and brightest poets, novelists, painters and architects, not to mention composers and photographers, provided them with room and board for a whole year.

Fred saw the gates open. He walked in. Stared at the magnificent gardens, listened to the clinking of glasses, voices. A soulful figure (out of a Lamartine poem?) came up to him, glass in hand and, in that ending day, glistening hand wet from ice cubes in her glass, said:

"Que fais-tu içi?"

"I'm just..." He stopped. Why had she barged in like that with such a naïve question, I mean, here she was saying: "What are you doing here?" when it was obvious that I was strolling in "her" garden! But she was torturously beautiful, now high on the perfume of her single malt scotch. He crouched down to help her find her contact lenses on the ground, slightly leaning into her back, and what a shapely back (a soft core flick he had once seen, in the old days, on 42nd Street, where the hero almost but not quite...)

"May I..." he said.

"Laissez-moi tranquille!"

Fred flipped through his mental dictionary. No help and so...

"Fuck it, mademoiselle, if that's the way it's going to be..."

In turn she turned around, looked at him, sighed and answered: "if that's what you want, follow me."

The marble stairs seemed to be going up to paradise (he hummed the movie song).

She stopped on the last floor, an aerie. Opened the door, beckoned to Fred.

The sperm-splattered sheets had yet to be removed, the bed straightened out, pillows punched so that they might look brand new.

She opened a small window. Undressed. Kicked the remaining sheets to the ground.

"Come!"

Her body was beyond description (a cliché if ever there was one!). She spread her legs, as if to invite Fred to do the same thing and, as he had previously uttered, "fuck her!"

He had a rough time slipping out of his tight slacks. His shoes. His socks. In fact, he took an infinity of time to find himself on top of her, his knees joined as if they had been twins born to be eternally connected.

He pushed (at least fifteen times.)

She uttered: Piu' Forte…Piu' Forte… in her recently mastered Italian.

He thrusted (let's say, at the very least, fifteen times) (She whispered in his ear: Godo, Godo, Porco…)

He exploded (difficult to be specific about the times his sperm emerged).

Not a word spoken. But a series of exhilarating gasps. His heart beat crazily. (He panted in her ear.)

To assure a secondary enjoyment, she sang the first line of the Marseillaise: "Allons enfants de la patrie…"

It must have been around 3:18 in the morning. The sun peered through the port-hole. She wanted to go to the W.C but heard the lock click down the corridor. She knew it would be too late were she to wait, so she took a porcelain pot from underneath the bed.

He: (Snoring loudly).

She: (peeing. Singing meza voice):

"Someone's in the toilet with Nadja,

"Someone's in the toilet I know…o o"

Then peed again in slower spurts.

No Kleenexes around.

She wiped herself with the corner of the sheet which, fortunately, had fallen onto the freezing marble floor. She then pushed back the porcelain pot, slid into bed without ever waking him up (by that time, because of the light, he had covered his head with a pillow and fell asleep).

SEX : THOUGHTS ON TIME

After sex: this may be the only experience that is definitely marked by a "perfect" recall. The body's memory, in such instances, is flighty. As E. M. Forster writes, exegetically, in Howards End: "Only connect…" The connection, however, is intense but fleeting.

We have an encounter (see above) without subtitles, a brief physically exhausting (when perfect!) but reasons does not reason in such moments. It leaves the body to itself in a language not privy to language.

Love you!

Love you, too!

And that's the end—the conclusion of bodies in conversation. On a minor scale, it's a hint of no lasting impact, quite like the body's autobiography and here perhaps a type of meta-memory?

We "make" love, if you'll excuse the following demeaning example, like we "make our bed" in the morning, after a pleasant "after."

"You're crazy! when I 'make' love, it's a metaphor, a sliding away from a physical truth, a moment's reality."

There is another thing we should consider: the perfume, I mean that lingering remembrance of someone. I can still retain a wisp of her on me as a musical phrase I keep on hearing, at least for a short time.

Even if you think you do remember, isn't it more like a series of disconnected photographs in a personal album? Flipping through it, a perfumed pictorial evocation might revive, for a second, a past affair, long shelved in the mind.

If you dream of love, would that engage you in a recapitulation of a distant experience? Or would you have both pleasure and impatience, trying to put a name, a body, eyes, a mouth to that fleeting or even repetitive, persistent dream? Did it ever occur, even if it were dreamt every other night, and for a whole week, would you, after all that, find her name? Where you met? What you ate afterwards? How many cigarettes you smoked?

Listen to St. Augustine: "The memory containeth also reasons and laws innumerable numbers and dimensions, one of which hath any bodily sense impressed..." (NY: E. P. Dutton & Co., 1950, p. 235).

Would we be victims of memory?

I suffer a sort of void, practically defined by Today. Yesterday disappears. Tenses are crucial here, they may be the last traces of the past.

Words are palimpsests without any canvas on top.

I begin and then, artfully, artificially, without a true passport, travel through a make-believe world.

We are illiterate children of Today with hardly a wallet filled with souvenirs.

Nobody tells the past.

At least we tend to believe that the narrator's "I" is still human rather than a grammatical invention (see Barthes). Maybe that knowledge fools us. Maybe we are like those straw enemies whom we so wanted to kill, straw ourselves?

Metaphors once more may help me discount the truth as truth, as an uncontestable fact. Sometimes we are auto-convinced that writing is a form of mimickry. Let's pretend! Are all souvenirs tricks of the mind? Are they pretenses? I am below a mosquito infested forest and my father hands me a cigarette and tells me that'll keep them away. I do not remember that scene or that voice. If my father hadn't told me and repeated it again and again, I would never have recalled the summer of 1937.

END OF SECTION

He dreamed of Paris. Saw the Eiffel Tower with its gleaming lights at night.

His only lead was to continue tracking him down, as if he were an animal in a deep forest.

His appetite haunted his stomach. He remembered (at least

that!) a "dolce" he had eaten in Rome for breakfast, three days earlier.

He saw him kissing a graduate student. Spoke on Raymond Roussel. Used a structuralist terminology.

"Any questions?"

In the back of the seminar room, someone raised his hand. "I don't understand a word of what you're saying. Remember, that novel hasn't even been translated into Italian and our professors are far behind in that terminology."

I had timed my talks. Fifty minutes for each writer and 25 minutes for questions, but I put all that time aside and provided the students elements of linguistics and structuralism.

I had found a beautiful room off Piazza Vittorio Emmanuele II, 00 185 Rome. I also had caused a hushed scandal. "Professors," a student warned me," have a half hour accorded lateness to class and here you show up on time! They'll never forgive you..."

As they talked, he went through the documents (by then that's what he called them) in the locker at 107 bvd Raspail.

Speaking of love, what about "Crimes and Misdemeanors"? A guy gets a killer to do "it" on his mistress, all along regretting that, if he hadn't done it, he would have lost his job and good fortune as a shrink.

A couple of years later, Allen asked him, sitting near a piano: "how is it (in the present tense) you don't seem to have any regrets? Doesn't the guilt seep through your memory?"

He dreamed of Paris.

Saw the Eiffel Tower.

(By the way, translated into an English setting, the plot is exactly the same as in "Match Point." At least that's what my daughter says.)

His only lead was to continue tracking him down. Here, he said to himself, I may have miscalculated.

He saw himself in late afternon kissing a beautiful but troubled graduate student.

I asked that beautiful but troubled student who had interjected the above opinion to go out with me and eat at a Kosher restaurant not far from the synagogue. She accepted.

"When do you find time to write all those seminars? Do you expect Bulzoni to publish them?"

Cats everywhere.

As they talked, he went through the documents (by now he called them "documents") in the locker at 107 Blvd Raspail.

Could it be that, by the greatest coincidence, both had been in Paris at the same time? A fragile possibility. He had taught that seminar in 1988 at the time he had begun his career as a lowly paid reporter. He had taken off two weeks to visit Paris. He then found a room on the rue du Dragon.

Across the street, a popular hang-out for poets. One day, as he walked by, he saw a man wearing a pin-stripped blue single grey breasted suit, probably bought years ago before that tailor went out of business.

I followed him to the Bastille, humming the zither theme from "The Third Man."

He jumped aboard a "bateau mouche" which went through the canal and, on the right, one could read "L' Hôtel du nord" in a Jean Gabin movie.

The taste of the "Dolce" wore off. He tumbled out of bed, still half-asleep, holding on to the remnants of his dream or was it a dream?

"This time," he said outloud, "I'll follow him wherever he goes."

I found a little restaurant in Campo di Fiori, not far from Trastevere and that (famous) old church on the corner. Spaghetti with garlic and oil. A bottle of Borsalino. An Insalata di Casa (tossed romaine lettuce, pomodori and a house vinaigrette).

Walking past the fountain right there, he took pity on a homeless fellow. He offered him a slice of bread and a piece of cheese he hadn't eaten.

"I don't eat stale bread. I hate provolone."

That was that for my humanitarian gesture.

I saw SG walking through Roman streets and often stopping to look at names on the buzzer of each apartment building.

I followed suit. When I got to the university, by chance, I ran into the dean of the faculty and said to him how surprised I had been at all those Italian names.

"Young man," he replied, "we have lots of Sicilians in Rome." As if they had just arrived from Africa (like Plato...). The dean was a Baudelairian specialist. In his translations of sonnets, for example, "L' Albatros," he found it useful to add two more lines, to inform readers of the "true" meaning of the poem.

But then again, why not? Is the author the only one to define his or her text? Some French philosopher had insisted that "authors" were dead and perhaps they were. After all, where did they come from if not from other texts, other cultural signs inhabiting them, probably without their knowledge. If they didn't receive a literary prize, instead of complaining, they all should be happy. Follow Sartre's lead when he turned down the Nobel Prize. All of a sudden (and that was the advantage), his sales soared. Everybody was reading Les chemins de la liberté, a multi-volume work Maurice Roche once told me, was his worst!

But then, I said to myself, sitting on a bench in the Tuileries, even so-called automatic writing represents an author, a signature. When André Breton condemned Tristan Tzara for having sold his "écriture automatique," Breton did not consider that every text written consciously or unconsciously (Groddeck's "ça") was unduplicable by any other poet and thus, in fact, signed as one could say that anybody's dream was a personal set of images. If Freud's The Interpretation of Dreams could decypher hidden meanings and make sense out of that screened-out significance, on the surface all dreams were the same. I would here, at the risk of falling into a trap, claim that dreams are reflections of their time and thus a dream in the Classical period will not be the same, outwardly, at least, as a dream in the Romantic period. The stage settings may change voices, too...

I thought of the Rauschenberg exhibit at the Met. First things first, I said to myself. He is what I see. The technique, the increasing red color, the sizes. And then, what? Well, I thought, he is revealing both his culture as well as the vertical one from the vulgar to the sublime; the personal: his mother's patchwork. The general culture: photos of Eisenhower and Lincoln stolidly sitting in his memorial armchair; photographs of Sixteenth Century classical painters etc., etc. Without being a Lacanian, there had to be a "back-up" to these works. And so I began working backwards. Texas, 1925. The huge State, in fact, a State within the States. This may have left an indelible mark and might perhaps explain the attraction of larger pieces, certainly much larger than the Paris school of painting! Then again, and let me repeat, the importance of the mother's sewing odd pieces of cloth to make herself a skirt from found pieces. Would that have been the first "found object" he might have retained deep in his memory? While in France, had he ever visited the Facteur Cheval's palace made up of rocks found on his bicycle route, delivering mail and later, that same afternoon, with a wheel barrow, go back and build himself a "palace" as well as his tomb?

But for Rauschenberg, the aesthetics of it all! The influences of DADA where, on a much smaller scale, chance words were strung together, much as the "cadavre exquis" for the surrealists. And, for that matter, but on a diminiutive level, Joseph Cornell's found objects placed in boxes?

All that, including the time he spent at the Académie Julien in Paris, seemed, retrospectively, totally negligible. One man's work is unlike any another's; the fact of collecting odd pieces in the garbage, for instance, does not in any way correspond to another artist doing the same (Richard Tuttle who, by the way, at least for me at least, invented invention founding it in "trash" and made it into his own self-made alphabet). The specialist in "combine" works kept drawers full of fabric, odd pieces etc., etc., which his assistants picked out and then he would set them either on wood, on canvas or anything he had in mind.

We are left with what we see.

Could the above be my way of avoiding my failure at explaining what I was doing to satisfy my editor's obituary request?

It's all a matter of identity. "Qui suis-je?" asked André Breton in the initial paragraph in Nadja.

When all hell broke loose in Moscow, my father, much like Tolstoy's anti-resistance attitudes (my father, as a young boy, had memorized large chunks of War and Peace, probably to distance himself from his home's insistance on celebrating Jewish holidays or memorizing Hebrew).

(No one spoke Yiddish in his family: too common, too lower class.)

Some of his classmates called him the Idiot in the Family before Sartre ever wrote his biography of Gustave Flaubert.

But what could be said about identity? How simple it all appeared in the mirror when you shaved. How difficult if not impossible to retrieve it when you walk down a street, came across yourself in a window display and an unknown individual, who looked just like you, stood a little distance away, but still etched out in that same store window? Someone who might have been there all along, just to make your identity seem inescapably Other? And, for instance, was he "himself" or the reporter whom he was now shadowing? Was he in reality my "doppelgänger?" In my eyes, I switched identities. I now became SG, the sleuth haunting Fred's every move. Was my memory cheating? Who would ever have thought, not even in a novel, that this sort of switch might occur? Or was I totally misled by a simple reflection in a store window? I said to myself, check out Ovid's Metamorphosis and that wondrous star which had previously been Julius Caesar.

Greyish clouds hung low and darkly menacing. Similar to a migraine's effect on me.

I've already hinted above at my new identity, as the stalker, as one who had defied my own self in order to become the Other.

Time elapsed. Cities too.

By Lake Geneva, a tell-tale acknowledgement of Jean-Jacques Rousseau's Promenade of a Solitary Walker. The lake was, as I imagined, placid, with only a couple of birds swooping down. Then a sudden gust of wind and ripples nearing the shore. Mountains in the background. Not a soul around. Perfect for a walk and revel in the surrounding botanical species.

I checked by notebook. Even though I had just left Prague, I thought it might be a good idea to get back there. He walked through thick curtains. Felt someone trying to rifle his backpack. Entered and went straight to the Reception Desk. Gave his name. Got his room number but before entering the ornate elevator, he asked the desk attendant why nobody stood outside the curtains to make sure nobody would be waiting there to rip off one of the guests.

"It's none of our business," the desk attendant replied, coldly thinking to himself that all Americans ask the same question.

Keys dangled from his hand, one of those overly heavy hotel keys you must leave at the front desk whenever you decide to go out.

Which he did.

He walked to Kafka's house on the large square with a huge memorial statue. Heard Chopin's Third Sonata that evening. Ate in one of the local restaurants where the menus were trilingual.

He ate a Wiener Schnitzel, a boiled potato, sauerkraut and drank a 16 ounce Czchuvar beer.

Back at the hotel, he went straight for the bar.

A fluffy blond, hair overly dyed. Very dark red lipstick menacing the upper lip. She stood there in spiked heels, a loosely tied blouse with a hand-embroided Rumanian motif.

Very tight slacks.

She stayed with him for three hours and requested U.S dollars for her work. Then got dressed and left. It must have been close to 2 o'clock.

Breakfast served from 7:30 to 9:30. He went to the large dining area. Took a plate, cutlery. Helped himself to what may have been the most outrageously huge breaking of a fast! Eggs, breads, "confitures," salamis, sausages, fruits, orange juice, coffee or tea: all of a very powerful nature.

I followed him through sooty streets to the bus terminal where he bought a ticket to Terezin.

Puddles. Wheels slushing through.

Bare countryside.

He sat next to a young woman, asked her how far to go before getting to the concentration camp.

"Sorry, I really can't help you. I've never stopped there."

I had asked the bus driver to tell me when we reached our destination, which he did, in English. A steady drizzle.

Flags waving. He entered the main office to get tourist information and then went on his own to visit the quarters where prisoners had been held before being "transferred" to Auschwitz.

"We never executed any one here. You can see for yourself," and he mumbled under his breath, "there are no gas chambers here. We're very proud of that." He smiled. "Wier Viele Amerikanische Juden who come here in busloads."

I followed him to the camp at Terezin where once a full orchestra with children singing had fooled a Red Cross delegation into believing that, unlike all other camps they had visited, this one truly seemed hospitable even to reading one of the newspapers printed right there.

Potemkin Village.

Hungry, he found a local restaurant meant for truck drivers. I watched him through a dirty window.

A large peasant soup with black bread and butter. Then another bottle of beer. Then goulash with lots of onions, overly paprikaed.

Was all of this endeavor totally meaningless? I almost regretted, having asked the question about Identity, whether I had just been fooling around like a private eye with nothing else to do but collect my wages at the end of the week?

A clear day. Back in town, we walked across the newly refurbished bridge with its slightly too gilded statues. I thought of Tzar Alexandre's bridge in Paris.

Tourists snapping pictures.

One with mother and children.

One with father and children.

One with mother and father standing next to each other beneath one gilded statue implanted on the bridge.

Newspaper stands. Sausage vendors. Weird hats.

That night, "spiked heels" returned, but this time stayed until the late morning hours.

Not far from the hotel a McDonald's. A subway entrance a bit further. At every corner money changers.

All of that made me remember a curiously funny experience, at least retrospectively. My wife and I were driving fast on a Sicilian highway. As we approached Catania, everything slowed down. A truck stopped in front of me. I had been forewarned. The windows of the car were nearly closed even though it was already very hot.

All of a sudden two kids on their bicycles fell to the ground, right in front of us.

Before you knew what had happened, my wife's wrist was sprained. A kid had managed to slip his hand inside the car and steal our identities, our money. I ran after them. To no avail. They knew the side streets better than the carabinieri. One of the local cops gestured to me from his open truck to follow, and his buddies laughed at us.

At one unexpected moment, his left arm stretched out, indicating that I had to turn into that street, which I did, and parked on the narrowest sidewalk you've ever seen, right in front of Police Headquarters. We entered. In broken Italian I told the front desk what had happened. He showed us the way to a dark room lit by a single bulb. (A film noir?) He sat behind a 1932 Underwood and began asking us what we had lost. One finger at a time, he clunked down the information.

Amazing how much we had lost! Actually, as both of us went on remembering everything that had been in that hand bag, it seemed to us we had forgotten a king size bed, newly purchased shower curtains, four pairs of Feragamo shoes, ties, a couple of Italian shirts and a beautiful sweater my wife had spotted in a window display in Venice. I convinced her to buy it even if it seemed to us to be hugely over-priced.

When he finished, he handed over the carbon copy. Unreadable. "If you can't make it out, then I'll give you the original."

"But..." I stammered, "how are you ever going to find our stolen goods?"

"We never do."

When we got to our hotel in Taormina, the front desk asked us for our passports.

"Stolen in Catania."

He snickered: "You're the third couple without passports!"

Saturday night.

I had kept my Barclay's phone number, just in case.

Saturday night.

"Hello, is that Barclay's travelers checks? How soon can I get mine back? Stolen this late noon and, according to your publicity, I can get them back immediately."

Answer: "The man who does it is closed for the week-end. Try him on Monday."

Reaction: "God damn it! What kind of a bank are you?"

Silence.

That evening, having borrowed cash from the desk attendant, we got into a small argument in a restaurant.

"Don't tell me you were ripped off in Catania! New York is a thousand times worse. Just because you're in Sicily, don't assume every other chap here is a born thief."

We ate our spaghetti con vongole and did not enter into open conflict.

After Sicily, and I cannot account for the geographical leap, we found ourselves in Dijon, visiting a handsome museum, admiring ornate ancient residences, then the crowded Main Street with that odd combination of elegant stores and a McDonald's.

His next stop was in the suburbs of Plombières-les-Dijon. Here was a small town. A modern post-office, a deserted chocolate factory and a CRS compound. You only saw those highly trained para-militaries when they jogged down to the river where, if you were lucky enough, you'd catch sight of a large canal boat tied to the side and laundry drying on the upper deck.

He knew that, at 74, rue de Vilars, there was a great translator of Hungarian poetry who was now working on a translation of Louis Zukofsky's majesterial epic poem, "A." He had by now acquired a considerable reputation as the co-founder of "Ulysse fin de siècle," then as a novelist and lastly as a poet. Once a year, his wife organized a major dance festival in town, having viewed and reviewed hundreds of cassettes submitted by companies as far as Canada. She had invited Trisha Brown.

A recurring question haunted him in this calm Burgundian ambiance: what would he have been had he stayed in Paris during the war? Who would he have been?

During the war his aunt and her two daughters left Paris to hide in the Creuze in a catholic family, still working the land (the family had been forewarned that if the "concierge" revealed their identities, the Gestapo, or the Parisian "gendarmes" would round them up, send them to Drancy and from there to a death camp.

After the war, he imagined he would have been sent to the famous lycée Henri IV, facing the Panthéon not far from the église Sainte-Geneviève where Pascal and Racine were honored. The church wasn't far from the rue Montagne St. Geneviève which, if you walked down, you'd reach rue Descartes.

My classmates were (well, nearly all!) to go to one of the "Grandes écoles" and thereafter lead the way for the French Republic.

Encouraged by my parents and lycée friends, I passed the entrance exam and was admitted to the prestigious "Ecole nationale d'Administration" (ENA). In my class were future leaders of France including Chirac, Villepin, Fabius, Ségolène Royal, now a presidential candidate of the Socialist Party, and François Holland, her partner (four children.)

My first assignment was as a director of the French Railway system (SNCF). In fact I inaugurated the TGV Paris-Avignon and later Paris-Lille.

In 1981, when François Mitterand was elected President of the French Republic, he held a red rose as a symbol of the Socialist victory.

I was then named Minister of Transportation with a fine office on rue St. Honoré across the street from the PM's residence.

I had a chauffeur-driven Renault 16.

I was invited to accompany Mitterand to Shanghai when contracts had been signed for the French to build a TGV out of Shanghai.

Great food. French wines tend not to travel well. We applauded when the St. Emilion was served in proper glasses.

An unexpected reshuffling of the cabinet and, without ever suspecting that I would ever be selected for a higher position, I was...yes, chosen the new Prime Minister.

In the meantime, I had married a very rich and stunning heiress to a perfume corporation with factories in Grasse. Its main office on the avenue Montaigne, not far from the Arc of Triumph.

Together, we purchased what is called a "gentillomière," a gentleman's castle. There, to my great surprise, 16 bedrooms and nearly as many bathrooms, a rarity in France.

What I most appreciated was the garage. As of that moment, with my wife's smiling consent, I began collecting post WWII convertibles.

The 1966 Ferrari.
Series III E-type (1971) Jaguar.
1960 Alfa Romeo Giuletta.
The 3000 MK III, 1964 Austin-Healey.
An MG TC (1960).
A Morgan with a Rover engine (1970).
And finally, a French-built Bugatti.

To make us less of a bourgeois family we purchased an early Raushenberg "combine."

To honor President Chirac's scandalous vacation, we too decided, along with our 2 year old daughter, her 4 year old brother and lastly, another daughter who had just passed her 10th birthday, to spend a quiet week on the Isle Maurice at a five star Le Prince Maurice. She payed for everything. A thousand dollars a day. We played tennis.

We ate like the president.

And then I divorced her. The settlement was favorable: I got to see my three children every other week-end. Spend vacations with them on alternate years. Buy them gifts for their birthdays.

I then married a famous TV hostess and adopted her four children.

We found an apartment at 21, rue Pauline Borghèse. There, I put up my three children. They got along famously with my wife's four kids.

We then moved into an Art Nouveau building facing the Bois de Boulogne; little did we suspect that, on the ground floor, there was an immensely rich art collector who quickly took a liking to us and suggested he would help us begin an art collection with small Eskimo statuettes. We bought ten. Placed on a large and low glass table in the living room, they immediately attracted attention. He then suggested we stay with the exotic and purchase Egyptian works. That we did with enthusiasm even though the pieces were monstrously expensive. (He had warned us that the Internal Revenue people taxed you on visible signs of wealth.) "Do not vaunt your collection or else..."

My "TV" wife had to be seen in public and so we often went to concerts at the salle Pleyel; seeing a number of plays at the TNP or the Comédie française. A bit exhausting but educational.

For the New Year, we settled back in the Gers where my wife had a fantastic residence. We invited ten friends to come along with us. The meal was splendid. Oysters with a 1983 Louis Reoderer champagne.

A Pâté de fois gras from the Gers, accompanied by a wonderful Meursault.

Ostera (French) caviar and here, I insisted we drink Grey Goose vodka. My wife looked up at me. "Stop drinking all those different liquids. Our guests will be totally smashed before the end of the "repas."

As a sign of my pro-Americanism (totally against current opinions!) Sarko and I decided to serve prime ribs, accompanied by my favorite 1978 Saint Joseph.

I love endives gently boiled and then slipped under the broiler.

I'll skip the rest, but when it came to desert, of course, we had a traditional "Bûche de Noël" accompanied by a local Armagnac.

The men retired to the library, smoked Havanas and continued drinking Armagnacs. The women retired to the large redone boudoir and did whatever women do on such occasions.

I later discovered my wife was cheating on me with an aristocrat in the countryside, much as in Renoir's "La règle du jeu."

Shortly thereafter we separated. I was allowed to see my adopted children every other week-end and on alternate vacations.

All I was able to keep for my own cellar were two cases

of 1978 Cheval (St. Emilion) as well as a case of Clos de Tart (Mommessin).

My life continued and perhaps having divorced my second wife, I was able to work much longer hours. That didn't last long.

Attending a reception at the Elysée, when I left, I was assassinated by an anarchist.

Newspapers around the world took notice as well as letters of condolences to my former wives.

Had I still been around, I might have asked for an addditional three crystal chandeliers.

With all those multiple activities, including a funeral with black flags hung outside my door (the French way). I had literally forgotten about my mission: follow Fred wherever he went. That had been one of my fondest dreams.

Memory! What shall I beckon you with? What classical metaphors and, why not, Giordano Bruno's De umbris idearum? I reeled at such comparisons since, as far as I was concerned, no learned allusions from Frances A. Yates were needed in this place.

I did evoke a lighter image and asked, once more, was there a gateway to myself? A site of return to someone within me whom I had forgotten?

A suggestion for this digression: was the "I" which I believed to be there, concealed, part of a Komar and Melamid exhibit? Could there have been a reverse immigration, patterned after my grandfather's travels, a brief return to Moscow before being once again sentenced to long years in prison in Siberia? His art of resistance had lasted briefly, but longer than Kerensky's regime. Was it a descent into an excess of morality?

Of a Lost Ladino in Siberia? Was it all a descent into excess morality?

Could this have been a story where I was a pawn, moved in a Stefan Zweig's novel, or in another manuscript which had yet to see the light of day?

The more I tried to elaborate, the more I waited, like Proust in his room with the blinds down, for some sort of annunciation, revelation of a mirage, the more I hoped to quench my curiosity. Again, as for me, "the 'imaginary' is simply what we have forgotten." (Marcel Cohen, In Search of a Lost Ladino, trans. By Raphael Rubenstein, Jerusalem, Ibis Editions, 2006, p. 40).

Would all these fruitless attempts, these fits and starts, lead to some resolution similar to a painter's resolve even if, for the viewer, like a zen-like Albers square, inviting the viewer into a contemplative world, nothing worked.

A pre-nymphet, out of Woody Allen's "Manhattan," attracted by what she had seen, suggested as an image a puzzle which had to be put together in order for memory to return, even in an esoteric manner, which she had recently read in the Kabbala?

Above, two thin black threads made of the sky a rectangular shape. There appeared all of a sudden as if a black sheet had been pulled over the whole sky, a momentary darkness. A minute later, a torrential downpour, lightning as a hysteric pounding, drummed into my ears.

Like a thousand transparent threads, the color of the sky quicky changed, allowing clouds to hurtle forward.

I thought of mountains of snow at 10,000 feet above sea level, looking down from an airplane port-hole.

Was it the same sky all over the world, without a care for us below? Or had it decided, all by itself, to defract the light and disturb my elucubrations and thus throw me off track, which I had so desperately tried to find?

The rain stopped. Nothing remained to testify to what had happened.

Back where I started from. (That damn circularity of the song!)

I forced myself to look elsewhere as if, doing so, all of a sudden some odd fact or feeling might generate the material I was seeking, answer questions I had asked myself.

An elegant gentleman, working for MI in a James Bond film, wore a spread collar, a light blue tie, with an expected lack of imagination since he had earlier on picked out a rather shocking red motif. You could tell his shoes came from Church's where they kept his size to facilitate his next visit.

Were these digressions meant to reject Fred within me or force me to constitute his being within me, to let me be "him" for the duration, letting me, as a matter of trial and error, have his friends, his family, his tastes in clothing, food and travel? His pleasures in life?

That may be the solution to my quest.

The idea sounded fine. However, what would I keep as a reminder of "myself" now "another?"

Once again, again and again, I summond up the same thought: would my memory desert me to become his?

Would my voice change? I did hope I might keep my mind as a disturber, allow me to keep moving through these subterfuges, modes of concealments, so that SG would never suspect my newly defined evasion and that, despite two deaths.

Now Fred speaks through me, finds more material in that ever-enriched locker in Paris which the concierge had allowed him to see. What he missed, and now I was privy to, were other lockers pushed to a distant corner and which, unbeknownst to him, held a trove of significant material, allowing me to write a far more precise obituary.

SG not only dressed well, had an important selection of ties hanging in his closet, shoes below, slacks hanging from rods, and a number of suits, some even double breasted, some meant for the summer and others for mid-season, and still others for winter's blustery requirements.

His mail had accumulated. He had thrown them all in one of those distant lockers: Mail from Columbia College, asking for money: letters from the Graduate Faculty of Arts and Sciences asking for money, letters from the Gay Man's Health Crisis, for money, from the Red Cross, for money, from "Médecins sans frontières," for money, from the Children's Federation, from the Preservation Fund, the Policeman's League, the NWACP, the TWU and even, god knows why, from an East Side Russian church, all asking for money.

Personal letters were tied together and, for the first time in years, someone would have the chance to read them. These were letters from his buddies in college, from his wife, when he had traveled, from his parents, when he had been stationed in Seoul who expressed fear every time a North Korean plane was shot down: "Are you close to the wreckage? Did anyone from your company get hurt? Where was your captain all that time and the sergeant, the evil one from Jamaica who tried to plunder your historian's mind?"

Love letters from Grace. Love letters from Jane.

Love letters from Cindy.

Love letters from Lizzi.

The list was quite impressive, but I decided not to read all of them. It would not have been an elegant thing to do.

Letters from acquaintances, asking if I were to be in New York during the fall break and other letters asking the same question for the spring break. Apparently he had kept up with lots of people all around his time in the world.

His curiosity was such that he decided to open one of those letters.

"Dear Freddy,

Where are you now and will you receive this letter in time to congratulate me on my forthcoming marriage? We had had such a fantastic time together, but when you went off on your wild goose hunt, checking out SG's every move, every acquaintance, every bit of his imagination, then I said to myself, you would never return the same as I had fondled you in bed on Waverly Place.

So take this as a very fond farewell.

Your Lizzie"

Approximately fifty feet away, where those lockers were to be found, Fred had missed a cache of SG's first drafts of his poetry and his prose and, for example, from "ANDORTHE" section I:

And
Proliferate a fish
On a menu
Tables empty
Join the ranks
Chewing in earnest
A Meaning
A melody
Our existence
Elsewhere
I think clear capacity
Curtains open unmasked
Retracting from hearing
Nothing
Is certain
Baffling radios
In uncertainty
Old rhetoric
A semblance of the past
Tropes overused
To cleanse memory
The "horror of explanation"
Or
Certainty blood cowering
Corners of New York
Uptown
"A lui seul" someone says
Maybe

Did not
All explanations seem
Worthless in your pocket
Dreams on the other hand
"und so vieter"
In that drama he was shaking
Hands with him
Self trying all the time
Rhythms as discovery
Solace in forgetfulness
Do not shave why undress
Vertiginous a gash
Gosh music once more
A blue book
Wittgenstein
numbers coupled
Resemble pain
Another life
Windows do not
Let light in
Manes, wise manes
A picket fence to keep them
all in mind
a syncopated abyss
open brain
a place of paper
this day
death isn't proud…

The finished ms. had not been accepted by any publishers (except Talisman) but letters of rejections were all carefully arranged in alphabetical order starting with the U of California Press (where he had published two previous books): "The Editors do not have the possibility of answering all the ms it has received, but we do regret not having considered your ms. Next time please enclose a SASE."

And here's another of the same caliber from Beachhead Press: "Sorry!"

Another from Paradigm: "The editors have enjoyed your work over the years, as have our outside readers, but at the present time we have promised twenty other poets publication of their work. If you are still interested in our press, please resubmit in three years. Yours, sincerely." On the envelopes he had written, in an impeccable handwriting, "Tough shit!" and then again "Up your collective asses!"

To change his mind, he decided to fly to NY and visit his family for the Memorial Day week-end.

"Dear Mom and Daddy,
Expect me early evening 'chez vous'! Keep some food on the table. We'll have breakfast together tomorrow morning. I'm going to buy my ticket right way.
Your son who loves you both."

Sitting at a table, outside the Rostand, sipping his espresso, he wrote the text of a telegram he was soon to send.

The Air France agency was next door.

"Bonjour, Mesdames. I would like to purchase a ticket for JFK, departure tomorrow. I have here my accumulated free milage sent by Delta, your Sky Team buddies. So far, over 100,000 miles! Could I be bumped up to business class?"

"Sorry. I can' help you."

Next counter. "Sorry."

Next counter:

"Well, it sounds encouraging but…(she hesitated in French) you'll have to buy a r-t ticket first. That's the rule…"

"'Merde, alors!" Why the hell does Delta mail me my monthly free milage accumulation?"

"It's not for me to answer. Please write to the Delta people in Alabama. Maybe they'll explain it better. 'Au revoir, cher monsieur.'"

And with that, I did purchase a ticket and found myself in tourist class the following day. At least I had an aisle seat. I often piss.

The smell of the warming up of those aluminium chicken or beef dinners was so vile that I decided to disregard the food and try to doze off.

Dozing wasn't adequate, as I lay dying of something.

But I did have an opportunity of giving in to a recurrent nightmare.

For some inexplicable reason I found myself in a hospital bed, attached to all sorts of glandular tubes stuck in my arm, actually on my taped-over wrist where the needle took care of me.

Every two hours the shapely nurse came and, in a small plastic cup, asked me to swallow ten small pills.

"I can't. I gag on Advil."

"You must. That's what's keeping you alive." (With a smile.)

She forced my mouth open and slid the pills down my throat.

"Now, swallow and be a good boy."

I had dubbed her 'Edible Ass.' Phonetically, it sounded better than "buttocks."

By that time, I had mastered lip reading. The doctor, who periodically came to see me, checked the chart, pinched my big toe and left. I saw him talking to the nurse on the other side of the glass partition.

"He's a goner."

"How long?"

"A couple of hours."

Indeed (as the Brits say) a few hours later I died. Just like the bed to my left, they covered me with a sheet and rolled me away.

Both our beds were immediately remade. Two other death

candidates were implanted there.

The stewardess woke me up. "American?"

"Yes."

"You must fill out the customs declaration and...be sure not to make a single mistake otherwise..."

"I got it." Have you... Have you...

Have you......

Signature.

Then I took out SG's manuscript, which had been gathering dust in the steel box inside a locker.

"It's always a pleasure to remember," wrote Gertrude Stein in her poem: "Hôtel François Ier (1931)"

So I flipped through the typewritten pages and soon fell upon the following passage, chosen at random.

"When I was a young boy, I loved words. I always thought they contained endless unravelings. Like bubble gum..." (The German Friend, NY: SUN, 1984, p. 140.)

TRAINS OF THOUGHTS

What did he say and was it only a transfiguration of sex?

He said nothing. I was throwing a flower away, a dead flower. Pay no attention. Noises everywhere. We live in a noisy ward. Operating room down the corridor.

I stopped. How come I've landed on that passage so accurately describing my own experience? With that, I put the pages back in the folder, probably bought in a nearby shop that sold books, pencils, pads, and watches.

Invisible SG sat besides Fred in the rented car heading toward New Rochelle. He got to his house around midnight. Went straight to the kitchen and found a delicious cold supper.

After breakfast next morning, he tried to remember everything he had seen, heard and touched in that house as if he had been a sniffing dog liberated from its cage. What had kept that house out of his mind? Never mind. He now felt at home.

Next to the kitchen, the dining room with a tiny wine cellar below the corner table. Then a large rectangular table. He immediately saw himself sitting there at a Thanksgiving dinner.

To the right, a bathroom. Paint pealing.

Then the TV room with a fold-away bed. Pictures of himself at graduation and the same for his sister.

Nothing had changed in the living room with that big bay window overlooking the next door neighbor's garden. His old Buick parked in front of his garage.

The rickety stairs he loved as a boy.

His sister's room. He opened her closet. Old shoes (all shined up) on the floor. Hanging from a hanger, her graduation dress when mother had saved enough to buy it. Baby shoes. Sweaters neatly folded. A couple of scarves she should have placed in one of the drawers of her commode.

Almost frightening, Fred thought how he could so perfectly recall every last bit of information about his house! What a memory! Or was it something which had always been there and only needed a good meal to set it off? In any case, he walked into his own room. Nothing had changed or was it just the image he carried within his brain?

A drum he used to play.

A dried-out flower he picked out of a Christmas vase.

Paperbacks. Mostly adventures bought down the highway.

All he could come up with was a French expression: "Au milieu du monde."

"Mi-lieu:" The world cut in half.

Then to corroborate that image, he saw once again the doll his sister had halved with an electric turkey knife. One porcelain eye still on the floor.

Was this her "Polyphemus" or perhaps her "Samson, eyeless in Gaza?"

Now, in the cellar. Trunks filled with old toys. This had been my childhood world, nearly expulsed from memory. All of it came back as if somebody had hypnotized me.

Peregrinations of the eye. A glance deformed.

Could I have invented, discarded, attributed signs where no signs were visible?

What had provoked the present? Were there secrets I had not yet acknowledged?

The next morning all of us went downtown to watch the Memorial Day parade. Only four veterans left. Two ambled. Two others needed canes. The High School band played what they had rehearsed for hours, John Philip Sousa.

On both sides of Main Street the police had placed barricades. But there was hardly anybody there looking and applauding.

The parade, as usual, went from the now defunct movie house down the street to that boarded mom and pop store where my mother used to buy her woolen spools for knitting Daddy's Xmas scarf.

When the parade was over, the four vets retreated to Dan's Dinner and sat in the back booth drinking coffee.

Veteran I: "I'll never forget when we entered Germany near Eupen and Trier on September 12, 1944. We then walked to Aachen with the First Army."

Veteran II: "I landed in Casablanca on November 8, 1942. We all cheered Ike when he was made commander-in-chief of all Allied Forces in North Africa."

Veteran III: "Speak of the devil! I was in Africa when Rommel's Afrika Corps won over Major General Lloyd R. Fredendall at Kassserine Pass."

Veteran IV: "I think I've heard all your stories before! You all seem to have such fond memories while I, in Bataan, in January 1942, just like in the movies, all of us were captured by the Japs. All I could summon up was our Norman Rockwell drugstore and all of us sitting at the counter sipping chocolate malteds."

We drove back to the house. Daddy fell asleep at the table.

Mom was in the kitchen making turkey sandwiches. Lots of Cokes in the fridge and a couple of beers.

All I really needed was to recuperate my bicycle helmet and charge down the street.

Can I call it my counter-memory? I can't be that precise, but I did know that knowing was never really on top of everything. There must have been, hidden in nooks and crannies, another world which I hadn't yet discovered, recovered. Why? They say those were the "good old days," when we remembered our high school sweethearts whom we later married, divorced and married again, got other kids, moved into a bigger house with a two car garage. What about clearing all that snow in winter with a newly bought snow removal machine? Or that first snow when we all ran out to get it on our coats. I got some on my glasses.

If the snow kept up, we made our annual X-mas snowman without forgetting the carrot for a nose and a top hat to dress him up.

A couple of weeks later, Daddy retired at the age of 65 as general manager of the B&Q market. This time we stayed home for a longer time (or so he believed); he asked if he could take my homework desk, stuck in the cellar, the one with two drawers on the right. Of course, we said. We carried it upstairs and placed it in the TV room, in front of the large window. That's all we ever got to know about what he did inside. Maybe he was twiddling his thumbs? Maybe once a week he called Buddy from the store.

Then he died.

We had a private ceremony for him in the town's cemetery. Sis came in from Topeka where she lived with her husband and three kids.

Sam, Buddy and Joe, all former vets. They came.

When Mom went to the bank, as she did once a month to get her social security, the bank manager asked her to come to his office, which she did. He said her husband had a secret account which now was hers. It amounted to $30,000.

As she tells it, she nearly fainted right then and there. With that cash she had the whole house painted and the roof fixed.

Where had he gotten all that money? It was now a bit too late to ask. She was happy to have it.

A while after having buried Daddy, we went into the TV room to clear out his desk and especially those two drawers. He had been there for over 20 years and we thought the place was a holy mess since he hadn't allowed us to clean it. Not even once.

Mom and me had a real surprise. In the top drawer I found a thick folder with bold letters on it:

MY LIFE
A Poem

I read it in one day. Mom came in: "What's it all about?"

"His life with all the ideas he had in his head plus all sorts of thinking about the nature of poetry. I'll never know where he got all those weird ideas, certainly not from those old books in the TV room, and he really never went to the public library right down the road. We'll leave it at that. Here's an epic poem he worked on for years."

The poem was a mixture of sonnets, essentially inspired by Shakespeare, pentameters, free verse, sestinas and any other formal, constraining mode of writing.

As for themes, there too he wrote about everything he had ever cared for: leftist politics, the Great Depression, and WWII. He also took violent exception to Ezra Pound's politics and his nutty economics. That was only a part of 'My Life.' What he seemed to care for the most was the English language. He was also deeply committed to quotidian elements: the washstand in the cellar, the dryer, the laundry line going from here to there. All of it made perfect stanzas and partitions.

Seen through his American eyes, British culture, encompassed by history specifically by Shakespeare's historical plays, held a real place in the poem which he quoted at times, reworked like he did with Pericles, Prince of Tyre. If you really wanted to get to the heart of Daddy's epic poem, you'd have to put on Elizabethan glasses.

To counter this personal reading, he also tucked us in: me, sis and especially mom. In fact, nearly every partition ended with "Mom, I love you." There was a tinge of the maudlin in all of this family business but it seemed necessary to establish a series of checks and balances.

He even included his travels. In the British museum, we walked so many miles that the soles of my shoes gave out and I had to buy another pair at Le Printemps when we got to Paris and there again, going through the Louvre, the same thing happened. We visited gothic cathedrals. Daddy had memorized all of Henry James's Chartres.

Then off to Verona. Daddy said, and I remember it well: "To hell with that couple!" but he did want to see Catullus's haunts.

By that time I had begun calling him Daddy.

In the semi-darkness of the bathroom, I read Carl Sesar's translations of Catullus, and especially number 32, so often eliminated from Victorian translations and frequently without even a mention.

"Come on, my little Ipsithalla sweet,
You delicious piece, a good girl
And let me take a nap with you
....
But just home, warm it up,
And spread out nine straight fucks for me."

You can see why Queen Victoria might have objected.
Mom knocked on the door.
I wrapped my Catullus in a large towel and threw it in the

laundry bag.

"What ARE you doing in there for such a long time?"

"Just thinking."

Was Catullus one of our greatest Latinate influences on Daddy's poetry? Perhaps his The Writing of Guillaume Apollinaire may also have been a factor in his work (by the way, SG had edited that work in a bilingual edition published by Wesleyan UP.)

In any case, upper or lower, it was Daddy's habit to fool all expectancies. The more I read, the surer I was that he had done more living, loving, collecting facts in his poem than he ever did in life.

When I was ten, I was convinced, would you believe it? When Mom went about her household chores, she too, in a funny way, was always writing a life-long poem. She sang when the Hoover went around the house; she hummed when her foot played with the Singer, and she spoke ever so quietly when she washed the dishes. She said it was a way of cleansing her head of all unnecessary things. That was the reason she left the dishwasher alone.

While all this was going on, I mean my reading and Mom's own poem, my sis was making out with her newly found boy friend, an old flame from High School. She knew her husband and three children would never find out. Kissing, tongues tied, hands moving down, hers on him, his on hers. With all that, were they actually duplicating one of Catullus's poems?

I too was on my way to sperming in a handkerchief, reading a magazine I had recently bought and kept hidden under my pillow. Purchased in one of those triple X's with a curtained door and, in large letters on the window:

Magazines
Sex toys
Party favorites
Booths
Live performances.

I never got further than the magazine racks.

SG slowly learned all about my life, dissected it as if I were a living cadaver with a personal history as a multi-volume book. I did find it amusing that a French professor had wended his way into my being, a mirror image of both of us, a body within a body, eye for eye, reflecting on my life as I had done on his.

Did he know more? Was he reading my life, my daddy's as a preface to a study of aesthetics and journalism, a presence of the daily in life? Was he being intellectually stimulated as an afterword, elucidating, perhaps even redefining a purer self, contained, an experience that only a biographer would attempt to make?

What he undoubtedly found commensurate with his own interests were parallel experiences: what Littré did for Francis Ponge. What Fowler's Modern English Usage was for Daddy.

Throughout his epic, he would religiously consult Fowler and at times quote his definitions, for example, Daddy was fascinated by "overtones" and "undertone."

Fowler wrote: "There is a difference worth preserving in the figurative uses of these words. "Overtones" are the higher notes… "Undertone" is not a technical term of music, though sometimes misused as one…" (pp. 430-431).

Why need to justify Daddy's thought when he believed there WAS a connection between poetry and music? (Hadn't Mallarmé suggested that in his Oxford speech?) For Daddy both "over" and "under" allowed him to decipher that dual movement in his verse, at least architecturally.

When he was still my "Father," I would see him sitting in the living room listening to Mahler or Casadesus playing Debussy.

When my Daddy deigned talk about poetry (never his own), it was a comparison between language and music. He disdained those French theorists who transposed analytical terms meant solely for literature to everything creative: music, painting, architecture, in fact, everything was syntax, grammar—something outside of its proper definition.

When Father wrote about politics, he also quoted Fowler as an exegetical treat:

"Women having the vote reduce men's political power." (p. 216)

Poetry shared that view. When one power gains a greater power, another one's diminished. This comparison was always carefully wrought—an intensity of language came to dominate themes, the latter unavoidably suffered which may explain—retrospectively—how Daddy tried insistently to establish a perfect though resilient exchange between his quest for the proper word, the proper rime, and a narrative passion where he developed his story line, characters, descriptions of snow, clouds, rain, filmic allusions and especially his fascination with the secret workings of memory.

He was equally fascinated by the relative immobility of human societies as reflected in art and, for example, what he called the persistence of comic strips starting with the Elgin marbles to the Bayeux tapestries, to marginal illustrations surrounding a page of a manuscript as of the twelfth century.

That represented a continuum, a transference to Batman or Classics Comics replaying with language and image Frankenstein, for example, with morality's decadence or war, poverty, cities, trade.

Let Mom quote the title of a fiction by Tony Eprile: The Persistence of Memory.

So many have rethought that lapidary formula that neither SG nor Fred believed it (except if you grew up in Brooklyn in a Hassidic neighborhood!). Memory is not a constant. Isn't it rather a selective filter? At times, indeed, we remember what, for us, was truly memorable, but even at that moment there were gaps. Something we reject, something which is dangerous to recall, a terrorizing memory, let's say, gas chambers. This allows us to doubly survive. We MUST forget. That is our passport to reality.

Such was not the case with Latin for Daddy. He was literally impregnated with it which he figures as an "undertone" in his work, together with Bede's on isosyllabic rhythm. All that mechanism to grasp the Truth!

That was the reason why he had on his shelves Balbusus of St. Gall's The Book of Sequences. Were not all works of fiction, including his own poem, founded on the concept of sequences? He also found Marbod of Rennes, De Ornamentis Verborum a priceless reference as well as in it's application? William IX, Duc of Aquitaine's early troubadour poetry, as well as those romances by Chrétien de Troyes : he read them all outloud. Did my sis or I understand anything?

Was the poet, to quote the Gospel According to Mark, "The voice of one crying in the wilderness?"

The question came down to this: was the silence of memory muzzled? That was for me the only description of my Daddy's behavior and one of the fundamental themes of "My Life."

"But why," I asked myself. Why this inability (or ability?) to talk about his passion and talking without hesitation about stews, summer vacations in Ct., being a grandfather, playing poker with those veterans who were still alive? Always the past, the recent past, the distant past. The present was always shrouded.

When Mom and I first entered his inner sanctum, from where we had been politely excluded, we tumbled over a thousand books we ignored as if, at night, we would never have suspectd a wheelbarrow, full of books secretly rolled into our home.

When I looked, I realized that whatever I remembered about Daddy was next to nothing: only a profile. However I was now ready to read, to tax my own memory, reach back and admit that my Daddy had led a double life much like those 19th century heros in French novels who, married, nevertheless kept a mistress in town with horse and carriage, a stipend, a seat at the opera, a warm physical relation (depending on the fellow's age) as well as a tattler's tall tales about the secret goings on in Paris and, to a slighter extent, out in the provinces as Mme de Sévigné had done writing to her daughter. But when the inevitable break occurred, both had to meet in secret places for a while before splitting apart. Still, at the Opéra one would observe the other through elegant binoculars.

A surprising collection, meandering, as was his epic poem "covering" so many topics, so many styles, so many poetic structures. At times even inventing them.

The library Daddy had accumulated was organized by topics, or almost so. The very first dealt with rhetoric and included, among many others, works by Cicero, Horace, right down to our own day with Roman Jakobson and Vladimir Propp. Wasn't it impossible to think, to organize one's thoughts, to illuminate one's text without rhetoric?

Then histories dating back to Thucydides to Charles and Mary Beard, not forgetting Arnold Toynbee.

For utopias, he had, as a sample, Thomas Moore, Rabelais to Fourier. For dystopias he included Orwell's Animal Farm as well as that enlightened marquis de Sade who actually relished in society's decadence as the only path to freeing man's nature.

As for poetry, well, that may have been the most extensive collection I've ever seen ranging from Li Po, Homer, Virgil, Arnaut Daniel, Chaucer, Villon to Dante not forgetting Ezra Pound's Cantos as well as his ABC of Plain Reading—a perpetual source of good sense!

Novels? They were organized by centuries ranging from Don Quixote to Mme de Lafayette, to Lawrence Stern, Diderot, and especially Flaubert's Bouvard et Pécuchet which he considered as significant as St. Thomas' Summa or Diderot's Encyclopedia.

There were no exits to this library. Surrounded by past and present, that food was amply sufficient. Truth, in fact, resided in conversations between those works. Why would anyone with a degree of common sense ever wish to leave such a paradise on earth? One could come up with any work—esoteric or traditional—and Daddy had purchased it, usually at a second hand bookstore or at the annual library's book sale. Take for instance Alice in Wonderland. If some readers believed it was meant for children as the Wizard of Oz seemed to indicate, they were way off the mark; One didn't have to share André Breton's incredible admiration for Lewis Carroll, whom he considered as the epitome of his cherished "marvelous." What was undeniable was that "Alice" must have nourished countless story tellers, liberating their imagination, freeing them from so-called realism.

In a huge paper basket he had bought at a flea market, we found snatches of ideas on paper which he had discarded so that, when we looked at them, if we wanted to, we could constitute a parallel poem. We didn't out of respect.

Daddy lived out of the detriments of that dust settling everywhere every time he left a book on the shelf for too long a time. Today meant nothing to him. But don't get me wrong. Daddy played basketball, liked throwing a football at me which I tried to catch, fell down, got up again and threw it back at him.

Daddy also loved sitting at a drugstore counter, wallowing in banana splits: chocolate, vanilla, and sometimes either coffee or strawberry and a thick pouring of a chocolate syrup. He loved Islay single scotch malt and looked down with scorn at NY State's version of Champagne. Only Reims would do!

Sometimes, when he was tired of working in the TV room, we would drive out to Westhampton Beach. He said if you walked a great distance, you'd get to Montauk Point. Westhampton now was all real estate country. Everytime a store went out of business, like "Shock," a bank took over, repainted it, refurbished it, added fancy lights, fancy leather chairs and lots and lots of computers. If you wanted to purchase an estate in France or England they had the proper credentials.

At least nobody had yet polluted the town with an endless chain of Duane Reade's.

Daddy insisted on Montauk, however commercial it had become. He saw himself, like another Hemingway, coming back from a deep sea fishing expedition with a 200 lbs tuna, and, speaking of Hemingway, he did not disdain For Whom the Bell Tolls, not even the movie version, but here his memory flagged. Was the hero Gregory Peck? Spencer Tracy? He knew Jimmy Stewart had gone to clean up Washington; that Betty Grable had entertained the troops in Europe as had Harry James with his faithful trumpet.

When Daddy couldn't remember, he slapped his thigh, looked at Mom and, probably every time she'd remember the person, the place, the season and the occasion.

What Daddy could do with his faltering memory was to name all threesomes in Hollywood, starting from the Three Stooges, the Marx Brothers, the three musketeers. Or the Hollywood Ten whom he clearly remembered since he considered himself as the arch ennemy of Senator McCarthy. That he could remember!

He could also recite opening lines of many of his favorite poets but he had to stop thereafter. Not even Mom could help him out.

Dredging up images, voices, themes, poetic constructs from the past, and without hesitation, he continued to write about his life. Day after day, behind closed doors, looking out the window as if there, inspiration would be forthcoming. He came up with words to match his desires.

In a while I'll speak about what else I read in "My Life" but now, just another comment.

He despised psychoanalysis. Still, there was something to be said about Joyce's stream… (William James, Principles of Psychology, 1890).

He could not stand Freud, Jung, Groddeck, not even Anna Freud or Julia Kristeva. Anything which artificially played on memory's past. It may have been ok for Dora but Daddy's muted pride prohibited him from that balancing act, a gymnast ready to tell all or to disguise all, just to make the psychoanalyst swivel his mental chair and check out in The Interpretation of Dreams, what the dream was all about, and, for instance, in Daddy's case, what was the concealed significance of his going up and down the stairs.

In the near darkness of a movie palace, with only exit signs lit up (a Hopper painting?) Daddy would dream of his last line and add another one if it came to mind. Movies seemed to kick off his enthusiasm. He always kept a little notebook, the way Allen Ginsberg jotted things down, jotted down what had come to the surface of his being. He thrived on those notes. In that way he fed "My Life." Did that correspond to Tristan Tzara's found words? Or Ted Berrigan's?

Freud? The darkness illuminated, the past slowly, mysteriously, in an esoteric manner, creeping up to the surface, but that was a technique, a strategy well thought out. In fact, in that movie house, what had hitherto remained tentative, unformulated in words, that is, not yet translated onto paper, a line of poetry, a light, a suspicion brought out an alignment of words, all able to do the work of the translator, this time totally faithful to the original.

Perhaps, for those who were not poets, whose lives were unidimensional, whose relation to reality was immediate, culturally bound in the present, and bits of the immediate past, insufferable to some, psychoanalysis was the key to the unlocking of the hidden text by way of clarification, finding a language to express it. For those who were speechless, who spoke without speaking, that remained a momentary answer.

Daddy had relentlessly criticized that Harvard formula: "Let it all hang out!" He even talked about it around the dinner table. He was furious.

"That's decadence in a word!"

Little did he suspect that in my high school kids had already tried LSD. One of my classmates, thinking he was the Flying

Dutchman, leapt out of a third floor window. He cracked his head when he landed. Little blood. But lots and lots of it when his veins split open. The others, especially at a party, smoked pot. They said it was an incitement to good sex, and allowed you to make friends--quickly. When people spoke soulfully about identity, having lost it, having had it diminished, like water flowing down the bathtub, we said, fuck it! Identity is like an Ellis Island disease brought over from some shtetl.

We smoked. We danced body to body or at a Tahitian distance.

Part of the reason may have been that we didn't pay our dues at the NY Athletic Club, that we didn't go on winter vacations to some sunny island, that we did not go to openings: theater, operas or galleries. Nothing like that tempted us!

If you were so hung up on identity, why not carry around your neck some dog tag with your name, blood type, religion so that, if ever you were found dead in the streets on the Lower East Side, where you bought your drugs, you'd get a proper funeral. At least mommy and daddy would take care of you as they had never done before...

Mom said that if you were really into identity, why not frequent Asiatics, Hassids, Afro-Americans, Hispanics, Gays or American Indians? She called it collective solidarity or communally shared but...and here mom insisted: provincial, cutting out all other cultures. Choose your identity and hold on to it. Write about it. Get it published. Talk about your eternal suffering, your minor joys during annual meal times, the thrill of dressing like your clan, etc, etc.,

As the saying goes, always give a sucker an even break!

WE NOW INTERRUPT THIS NOVEL
Our correspondent Jonathan Izzy is standing
By Hadassah-Ein Kerem Hospital in Jerusalem.
Jonathan, what's the latest about Prime Minister
Ariel Sharon's health?
Difficult to say with any certainty
But as I'm sure you've already heard
Ariel Sharon suffered a huge brain
Hemorrhage on his farm and had to
To be air-lifted to this hospital. The operation
Lasted seven hours. Blood was removed from
His brain. If he comes out of it, doctors tenta-
tively believe he may be paralyzed from the
hips down. In Israel the mood couldn't be
Somberer. I went to the Wailing Wall to
Interview a couple of citizens. The first was an
Elderly Polish emigrant. She said, and I
Quote: "I'm destroyed. I didn't side with him
On the withdrawal from Gaza, but he is a
Remarkable leader, and I would certainly have
Voted for his new political party." A young man
Said: "This is one of the most dramatic nights in
Israel's history." My last interviewee said:
"Israeli politics is in turmoil."
If there is any further news about Sharon's condition,
I'll let you know immediately."
"Thanks, Jonathan."
Now back to our scheduled
　.....″

After that broadcast, I now hope to cheer you up! I've just found in that second basket, under his table, scribbled notes that, I'm sure, he would have at a certain time incorporated in his "My Life."

"Now," said Mom, "I know why he got up so frequently during the night. He said he had to go to the bathroom, but now, retrospectively, I can assume he had an idea or a line of poetry haunting him. He had to put it down. He left my side at least three times a night. He said he was a urine factory.

Now I can figure out why he was so grumpy, especially after the New Year! When I did suspect something was going on, I said to Daddy, 'why don't you go and see a doctor?'

"Mom, I've got breaking news! I was totally taken aback when I read it. Surprise isn't the word for it and you'll be in a state of shock when I tell you what I read in those throw-away notes and I quote: "My great grandfather was born in a shtetl on the periphery of Odessa on August 16, 1861." Odessa at that time, and who knows how it is today, had a population that was half Jewish. Half of them rich merchants whose wives wore Astrakhan jackets. Others lived in poverty.

Imagine Odessa. See Eisenstein's Potemkin. See those magnificent steps going down to the sea. See the baby carriage going down, faster and faster! Read Isaac Babel.

Walk through Odessa, smell the water, the shops, see the people hurrying about their business. Was it 1922 when the Great Famine hit that city? It seems that people always die, whether in a hurricane, a car accident, a famine or...war. Read Grossman and his articles for the "Red Army" newspaper. His interviews, so fantastically accurate that the editors censured them.

Now walk a couple of miles to a far less sumptious shtetl. The roads were not paved. Carriages moved along, pulled by horses or donkeys. Children wore their yarmulkes, played in the streets (sometimes, without any parent seeing them, they ate candies) but most often they studied Talmud.

Older men with black fur hats, long beards, sideburns, white socks (don't ask me why), and long velvet coats.

The women shaved their hair, put on scarfs. Cooked cabbage with potatoes and when they could get some, meat from the Kosher butcher. Ate Gefilte fish and latkes. We, I say 'we' because...one of those old men may have been my own great grandfather, born on August 16, 1861. Yes, Mom, my great grandfather was a Jew, drinking tea from a samovar.

The family religiously attended circumcisions.

Helped pay the mohel.

Attended Bar Mitzvas.

They went to marriages (divorces are very very difficult to get even when the wife is barren).

Did my great grandfather wear phylacteries on his left arm and on his head and prayed in the mornings?

They celebrated the Sabbath.

Shawls at funerals. Recited Kaddish for a whole year.

At home, the older son spoke Yiddish. In temple, Hebrew.

When he traveled out of his Chagall-like village, there were no flying cows he could wave to: no fiddlers on the roofs.

Yosef had the itch to travel and so he went to Odessa where he found a distant relative who got him his first job in a bagel factory. He then went on to matzos.

For an inexplicable reason, he was blamed for a petty robbery in the factory and shipped off to Siberia.

Out of this cross between Babel and Jabès, another young man stepped forward at the police station and admitted he was the thief. Yosef was freed (a rare deed for a tsarist regime). The guilty one replaced him for ten years of hard labor.

Then the tzar appointed Pobiedonostzvev, the most rabid anti-semite you could find. He had a clear program as far as Jews were concerned. One third converted, one third allowed to emigrate and lastly, one third to be massacred.

These so-called unpremeditated riots, now called pogroms, first hit Odessa on May 15-17, 1881.

Four thousand Jews came to New York. Eventually they scattered all over the country.

Yosef was part of the last third; he escaped while his village burned down. Not even his parents survived.

Yosef took an overcrowded ship, passed through Ellis Island, walked in total freedom on the Lower East Side. He was greeted by no other than that famous American Sephardic Jewish poet Emma Lazarus: "Welcome," she said. She took a liking to this young man, found him a room on Orchard Street with an overhanging light bulb and a bed. The toilet was down the hall. He spoke no English. But his Yiddish got him far. He loved his next door neighbors in his four floor walk-up. Because of Michael Heilprin, he got a job in a bialy factory.

Once again, as if the first time hadn't been enough, he was accused of stealing bialys and selling them to his neighbors at cut prices.

To escape prison, he took a train and settled in Topeka.

He married a shikse. Had three boys, all properly circumcised.

When Yosef started his new life, he changed his name to Y. Cobb.

When his oldest son got a travel itch he found himself in New Rochelle, a town named after one of the great Huguenot struggles during the Wars of Religion. They had been persecuted, they had been killed and so had his family, so he took an immediate liking to his new-found neighbors.

He got a life-time job at B&Q food store.

Had three sons: Shlomo, Abraham and David. Shlomo changed his name to Solomon. In school, they called him "sol."

What Daddy only began suspecting, years later, was that he too was part Jewish, something nobody had ever dare reveal. Oy!

What Daddy also found out, during his google search in post-Soviet archives, was that Yosef had been momentarily put up in rabbi Minor's apartment.

Finally, Daddy understood, and because he was able to jot all of this down, he said that I had a distant cousin named Serge

Gavronsky.

As it turned out, we had momentarily met in college, that very professor of French literature I had been assigned to follow in order to fill out an informatively bland obituary.

When SG died, he lay there in his bier on the West Side in a Jewish funeral home.

His close friends, colleagues, relatives all got up and said something sad, something humorous. They remembered his teaching evaluations; his prizes, his awards, his writings, his speeches, as if all of that amounted to a man's life...

That's the reason I wanted to attend his burial.

In a limousine going to the cemetery in Woodstock, I sat next to his best friend, David Gordon, who had flown in from San Diego for this memorial occasion.

For most of the trip, out of sadness and deference, we hardly spoke. After a while, though, we did begin to reminisce. David recalled, as if it were yesterday, how he had arranged a poetry reading for SG at the First Born in the vicinity of Columbia. It failed because the girls from Barnard thought 111th street and Amsterdam Avenue was too far to go. On the other hand, Bloomingdale's was right around the corner.

At the burial site, nobody recited Kaddish.

I guess everyone had forgotten that he had had a great grandfather who had been a rabbi.

If history is our memory, why remember? As the Zakhor says in Hebrew and translated into English:"Remember!" That was an imperative. But who remembered?

Now the coffin is lowered
Now the men use their shovels
Now hats are pulled back
Were they waiting for a tip?

Somebody sang
Somebody read Chekhov
A couple and then another
Left in their rented cars

The weather changed
Dry as snow weather
On Clover street sandwiches
Tea and coffee

The wind rose
Mountains seemed
To move strips of water
From the Shokan Reservoir

A rabbit ran across the road
A deer tied to the front of
A car.

He is survived by his wife of fifty years, his daughter, and two grand children, Antonia and Olivia.
 Had all of this only been a dream memory?
 When all is said and done, there may still be an ounce of hope to quote Steven Rose: "Our memories are recreated each time we remember." If I remember correctly I have used "remember" more than numerous times and so…
 Or to put it in another voice, when this novel is finished, will its language die or will it be remembered?
 Like an aging adult, could it also have been a slow death of memory?
 Perhaps nobody put it as succinctly as Steven Rose: "Our memories are recreated each time we remember."
 P.S. Andy Warhol: "I forget what I said the day before and I hope to make it all over again." (Stockholm, Modena Musset,

1968 n.p.)

FINAL QUOTE
"...I would make as if to put away the book which I imagined was still in my hands... Marcel Proust, Combray (NY: Modern Library, Vol. I, 1998) p. 1.

www.ingramcontent.com/pod-product-compliance
Lightning Source LLC
LaVergne TN
LVHW032005070526
838202LV00058B/6309